WHY I HELD YOUR HAND

YOUR HAND

Augusta Reilly

CHAPTER 1

Laura awoke to find a twelve-year-old boy in a baseball cap staring at her through her open car window. He was wearing a frilly pink 34D bra over his Little League jersey. It was her first clue that this wasn't going to be an ordinary Monday.

She had been awake now for about ten seconds, and what she'd figured out so far was this: she was lying in the back seat of her car in a parking lot somewhere, her bare legs dangling out the window and the skirt of her long yellow sundress bunched up around her hips. The top of her sundress was partially unbuttoned, and her hands were under the fabric, happily resting on her breasts. She wasn't sure how she'd gotten herself into this situation, but she knew she'd managed to do it without the help of drugs or alcohol, which somehow made it worse.

The arrival of a second spectator at the scene was her next clue that something wasn't right. A dark-haired young man wearing a grey suit and tortoise shell glasses was suddenly standing beside the boy. He was smiling. "Hello, Laura," he said, looking incredibly happy to see her. "So sorry I'm late. There was an accident on the interstate."

She had no idea who the man was, why he was apologizing to her, or how many of his old college buddies he would share this story with later. "I forgive you," she said. "Could you please ask your son to give me my bra back?"

"Him?" the stranger said, thumbing to the boy at his side. "I've never seen him before. I thought he was a friend of yours." He turned to his fellow spectator. "Jeffrey," he said, "could you please give the nice lady her bra back?"

The boy, motionless until now, turned and bolted across the parking lot.

"Sorry," the stranger said. "If you want, I can chase him down and wrestle the bra off of him, but I don't know how I'll explain myself to the police."

"How did you know his name?" Laura asked, suspicious.

"It was on the back of his uniform."

"How did you know my name?"

"Parking pass," he said, pointing at her windshield.

"And why are you so happy to see me?"

He looked at her chest.

"Besides that," she said.

"Oh, sorry. I didn't introduce myself, did I?" He extended a hand through the window. "David Harper. KPS Marketing. I'm your ten o'clock appointment."

And suddenly she remembered. She was in the parking lot of the North Powell town hall. It was Monday morning, June third, and she had a meeting with KPS Marketing. She'd been preparing since eleven last night and had come out to her car about an hour ago to take a power nap before the meeting. KPS represented some of the most luxurious (and expensive) travel brands in the country, and she represented one of the most unglamorous (and broke) tourist towns in the state. As such, her top priority was to make a good first impression.

Well, she'd made an impression, alright. She supposed the proper next step was to accept David's handshake. But both her hands were still otherwise occupied.

"Sorry," she said, still on her back. "I've been here working since last night and I came out to my car to take a little nap before the meeting and took my bra off for comfort and . . . you know what?" she said, interrupting herself. "I can't really think of any way to get myself out of this situation in an intelligent or dignified manner, so I'm just going to stop trying. Could you please spin around for a second while I freshen up?"

"Of course," David said.

While his back was turned to her, she sat up and quickly buttoned her dress. Smoothing out her skirt and combing out her long red curls with her fingers, she grabbed her briefcase from the front seat and stepped out of the car.

When David turned around, Laura's hand was extended and waiting for him. "Thank you so much for coming all the way in from the city," she said. "It's so nice to meet you."

The plan was to pretend this silly little semi-topless moment had never happened. But evidently, he wasn't going to let her off the hook that easily. He did not accept her handshake. Instead, he looked around to make sure no one was watching.

"Listen, Laura," he said, "I'm pretty sure I'll never have a better 'first time I saw your mom' story than this, so all I ask is that you think about marrying me. You can give me your answer after the meeting."

She laughed. And felt an enormous wave of relief. Making light of this extremely awkward moment was much better than pretending it wasn't there, and she was grateful to David for handling it with tact and humor.

"The twins and I will need to discuss your proposal in depth before we give you our answer," she said as they finally shook. "I'm sure you understand."

He responded with a laugh that seemed genuine, and he suddenly seemed more handsome than he had two minutes ago. It was the smile. He looked nice. She especially liked his glasses. He looked smart. He appeared to be about thirty, a good age for a man. Old enough to be responsible and committed, but young enough to be fun and exciting. And in this case, available. She'd noted his ringless finger when they'd shaken hands.

"Let me carry that for you," he said, taking her briefcase.

Walking across the parking lot with him at her side, she judged that he was about six feet tall to her five-foot-one frame. Tall was good. As was gentlemanly.

Speaking of gentlemen. "Weren't there supposed to be two more of you?"

"James and Spence," David said. "We came in separate cars. They're already inside."

"Oh my gosh," Laura said, trotting up the front steps of town hall. "I'm so sorry. I had no idea anyone was waiting for me."

A minute later they entered the conference room, and Laura took her place at the head of the table. To her left sat a freckled redhead who could have been her long-lost twin from the old country, only better dressed. He wore a neatly pressed blue suit and was pulling something out of his four-hundred-dollar leather briefcase. When David sat down beside him, the two of them together looked like the cover boys of *Consummate Professional* magazine. Across from them was a young man with disheveled sandy-brown hair and no tie who looked like he'd wandered into the meeting by accident during a sleepwalking episode. Other than twirling a pencil, he showed few signs of life.

At the opposite end of the table sat Carolyn, North Powell's mayor. She looked like a bitch, because she was one.

Laura put her twenty-dollar acrylic briefcase on the table and jumped right in. "So sorry to keep you all waiting," she said, extending her hand to the redhead. "Laura Delaney. Director of Economic Development."

The man stood up and accepted her handshake. "James Murphy," he said with a friendly smile. "VP of Strategy. We talked on the phone. Always a pleasure to meet a fellow ginger."

The sleepwalker stood up next, barely making eye contact as he extended his hand. "Spence," he said, not offering up a last name. "Creative Services."

She was already late, so she got straight to business once everyone was reseated. "I know you gentlemen are very busy, so I'll jump right in."

Her text tone pinged and she looked down at her phone. It was from Carolyn.

> *Love your boobs. Thanks for sharing them with us.*

She could feel her Irish face turning red. If Carolyn could tell she was braless, so could everyone else at the table. But she didn't have time to be self-conscious. This was KPS, and their time was valuable.

"So," she said, launching into her prepared speech, "as James and I discussed last week, for almost sixty years, North Powell was the most popular tourist town in the state. We were known for our quaintness, our Victorian architecture, and our charming main street."

"Really?" said David. "The most popular in the whole state?"

"During the holidays, yes," she said. "Our family-owned businesses earn thirty percent of their entire yearly revenues between Thanksgiving and New Year's."

Her text tone pinged again. It was Carolyn.

> *Are you wearing underpants or is that too professional for you?*

She'd respond to that later.

"I own one of the shops on Main Street," Laura continued, turning her phone face down on the table, "and I can personally tell you that the Christmas season is integral to my business's success. Unfortunately, we're smack-dab between Haven and Bainbridge, and everyone in the state knows, in the last ten years they've gone from small ski villages to two of the most popular resort towns in the entire country. They're slaughtering our local economy, so we've finally decided to hire a marketing firm, because, frankly, we've tried everything and it just keeps getting worse."

"Just curious," David said. "There are a million marketing firms that specialize in tourism. What made you decide to contact KPS?"

"Andrew Roth from Birch Hill. He gave me the name of someone at KPS who he said did a really great job." She picked up her phone and started scrolling through her texts, looking for the referral. "Okay, here it is. Spencer Markham, Director of Creative Services." It took her a minute to register the name, but then it clicked. She looked at the sleepwalker. "That's you, right?"

Spence raised a single finger. It was his entire response.

James chimed in. "You'll have to pardon Spence. If you're thinking he's spent this entire meeting with his head in the clouds, you're right. He's our resident dreamer and best idea guy, and what he lacks in social graces and fashion sense he makes up for in creative skills. Believe it or not, you'll have a lot of fun working with him. I, on the other hand, am a little less exciting. I'll be your chief demographics analyst . . ."

James blathered on some more about statistics and logistics and a bunch of other stuff Laura couldn't care less about. She was in a hurry to get to more important topics. "And you, David," she said when James finally closed his mouth, "what would your role be?"

"Well," David said, "if you decide to go with KPS, I'll be your project manager. So I'd be working with you every step of the way—"

You're hired.

"How much is this going to cost?" said Carolyn, bringing the pleasantries to an abrupt halt.

"I'll be liaising with our finance team to prepare three quotes," David said. "When we're marketing a tourist town such as yours, the low end is usually about three million dollars. The high end, not more than ten."

Dead silence followed. A few moments later, it was broken by Laura's text tone.

She turned her phone faceup.

I take it back, bring on the boobs. They're our only hope.

Laura decided to ignore Carolyn's advice and leave her two most persuasive arguments inside her dress. They'd already shouldered more than their fair share of the workload today.

She returned her focus to David. "That's a bit higher than we were hoping," she said. "Our max budget—"

"We could sell the whole damn town for less than that," Carolyn said.

Laura smiled at her guests, trying to keep the conversation friendly. "Our max budget is a hundred thousand."

"I knew this was a waste of time," Carolyn said as she stood up and walked towards the door. "Nice meeting you all."

The door slammed behind her.

Laura sat down. "You'll have to excuse Carolyn," she said. "She won the election by playing rock paper scissors and hasn't quite mastered the whole political charm thing yet."

But no one was looking at her. They were looking at each other, trading glances back and forth and mouthing silent words. She couldn't read their lips, but she assumed they were all saying something to the effect of *How soon can we get the hell out of here?* She saw David mouth "Yes?" to his coworkers, to which they both responded by making an OK sign, which she took to mean, "Yes, let's make a run for it."

"I do thank you all for coming out here today," she said, eager to end the public humiliation. "I'm really sorry our budget—"

"We'd like to bring the information you've given us back to the office," David said. "We can have three quotes to you by Thursday."

She said nothing, momentarily stunned. "Seriously?"

"KPS takes on a small number of what we call 'goodwill' clients every year. That doesn't mean we'll work for free, but it does mean that you could retain our services at a greatly reduced price. I can't make any promises, but I can assure you that James, Spence, and I will make our best efforts to persuade management that North Powell is a worthy candidate for the goodwill program."

"Okay," she said, still digesting this potentially great news. "I mean, thank you. Thank you very much. Thank you."

She sounded like Elvis. What an idiot.

"Our pleasure," said David as the three representatives of KPS started gathering their things. James and Spence said their goodbyes and departed.

But David remained. "You mentioned you owned a shop here in town," he said. "I passed a shop called 'Creations by Laura'. Is that you?"

"Wow," she said, impressed. "You're observant. Yes, that's my shop."

"I saw some kind of knitting kit in your display window—"

Her text tone dinged from inside her bag.

"Did you need to see who that is?" David asked.

"It's Carolyn telling me what a loser I am," Laura said. "Anyway, the knitting kit?"

"Right," David said. "My mother's birthday is this weekend, and knitting is her latest passion. Is it okay if I drop by the store and have a look at it?"

"Sure," Laura said. "But the basket you're talking about is a beginner's kit. I'm happy to put together something more level-appropriate."

"Well, she just started knitting last month and so far she's made me a square, a rectangle, a parallelogram and a rhombus. All pink. They were supposed to be ski hats but I can't get them to stay on my head. And also, I don't ski. And also, it's June. So yeah, a knitting kit that requires a minimal amount of effort and common sense is perfect."

"I think I can help you out," she said, laughing. "Are you the primary victim of her knitting?"

"I am. I have been her victim on many levels for thirty-two years."

"Meet me at the store in fifteen minutes. I'll get you that basket and we'll pick out some new yarns for you."

"Great," said David. "See you in fifteen."

He departed.

She grabbed her phone and looked at Carolyn's text.

It was a boob emoji, because evidently such a thing existed. She read the message that followed.

> *I just got to my car and my idiot nephew is sitting in the passenger seat wearing a pink push-up bra. Any idea where he could have gotten it?*

She turned off her phone. Little Jeffrey could keep the bra. She had plenty where that one came from, but there was only one David Harper, and he couldn't be replaced for forty dollars at Victoria's Secret. If she played her cards right, she might never have to feel herself up in the backseat of her car again.

CHAPTER 2

The closest parking spot she could find to her shop was at the very end of Main Street. If KPS decided against a goodwill offering, maybe the town could use their hundred-thousand-dollar budget to build a small parking lot for shoppers. Lack of parking was a very common complaint among tourists, as were the potholes that hadn't been properly repaired in over four years. Or maybe they could use the money for something non-tourism related, like fixing the roof on the high school gym or rehiring the elementary school art teacher.

As she walked to Creations by Laura, she passed the boarded-up Braincraft Toys & Games, remembering all the times she'd shopped there with her mother as a little girl. Candy's Candies was abandoned as well. Back in the day, it had been the most popular spot in town for birthday parties. But now all that was left of the once bustling shop was the letter "C," and it had been out of business for so long that even the boards on the windows were falling apart. Of the seventy-eight storefronts on Main Street, a full fifteen percent were covered in plywood. Even if KPS offered their services for one hundred thousand dollars, it was hard to imagine that it would be enough to turn North Powell back into the idyllic mountain village of her childhood. Frankly, it probably wasn't even enough to fill the potholes.

But there was no turning back now. She was only steps away from her store, and David was already there.

"Sorry to keep you waiting," she said as they walked through the front door of Creations. "Give me a minute. I have to climb into the display window to get the knitting kit."

Slipping out of her shoes, she tiptoed to the far wall of the display window to unhook the basket she'd put together for beginning knitters. "This one, right?" she called to David, who was in the corner looking at the course brochures.

He turned around. "That's the one."

She climbed out of the window.

"Here you go," she said. "Let's go find some yarns."

He followed her to the back of the store.

"Let's see," she said, picking out a tan yarn and holding it next to his face. "No," she said, "too light." She held up a dark brown yarn next. "Too close to your hair color. Let's try black." She held up the black yarn and took a long look. "This is nice," she said. "I like the black against your blue eyes. And the speckles in your frames. This is the one. It's on the house."

She immediately felt ridiculous. David had tentatively offered to charge her two point nine million dollars less than his usual clients, and in return, she was offering him a spool of yarn. "You know what?" she said. "It's all on the house. My very, very small way of saying thank you for coming all the way out here and taking the time to meet with me."

"I appreciate the offer," he said, "but I can't accept gifts from clients. Corporate policy."

"Alright, then," she said, disappointed that her own goodwill gesture, small as it was, had been rejected. "Come to the register, I'll ring you up."

"My mom actually lives nearby," David said apropos of nothing as he handed her his credit card.

Laura looked up at him. "Really?" she said, incredulous.

"You seem surprised," he said.

"I am. In North Powell there's no such place as 'nearby.' Unless your mother lives in a tree in the middle of the forest."

"She has a condo in Bainbridge."

"Ah," Laura said. "Nice." The entire town of Bainbridge was one of her worst enemies, but she wanted to be polite.

"It's the worst place on earth," David said. "I can't stand it there. But my stepfather died in January, so I've pretty much been my mom's date every Saturday for the last six months."

Laura felt a jolt of positive energy. She had a feeling she knew where this conversation was headed. "I'm sorry to hear about your stepdad," she said, hoping to rush through the condolences and get back to the part about him being only a half hour away from North Powell every Saturday.

"Thanks," he said, "but I barely knew him. They'd just gotten married the summer before."

"That's awful," Laura said. "How's your mom holding up?"

"She was the sole beneficiary of a two-million-dollar life insurance policy. Buying a seven-hundred-and-fifty-thousand-dollar condo in Bainbridge two weeks after the funeral really seemed to speed up the emotional recovery."

Laura laughed, then steered the conversation back to the topic of David conveniently being in the neighborhood every weekend. "So," she said, "how do you and your mom keep yourselves entertained on Saturday afternoons?"

"We watch *The Golden Girls* on her new seventy-five-inch flat-screen TV."

"Anything else?" she said.

"No. That's it. I've watched *The Golden Girls* every Saturday for the last six months."

Laura politely placed her hand in front of her mouth—as if that was really going to hide the fact that she was laughing to the point of shaking.

"It's okay to laugh at my pain," David said. "My stepfather's been doing it from heaven for six months."

"I'm sorry," Laura said. "I'm just picturing you sitting on a sofa with a pink rhombus on your head watching Dorothy and Rose eat cheesecake—"

"—when I should be spending my Saturdays outside frolicking in the sunshine like a normal thirty-two-year-old man?"

"Well," Laura said, tired of beating around the bush, "if you ever need to wind down after an exhausting day of sitting on the couch, I recommend an evening in North Powell. Most of the shops and restaurants stay open until at least ten and there are free movies in the park. And about a million places to go for a long walk or to watch the sunset."

"So is that what you do on Saturday nights?" David asked. "Watch free movies in the park?"

"Me?" she said innocently. "I usually go home, eat a frozen dinner, and then sit on the couch and read."

"Really?" David said. "On a Saturday night? No boyfriend?"

"No," Laura said. "Not for about two years now. Twenty-two months to be exact. You?"

"It's been two years and one month since I last had a date." He grabbed his chest like he was having a heart attack. "God, it's so much worse when I say it out loud."

"Well," she said, "if you should ever find yourself in North Powell after a visit with your mother, feel free to give me a call. I'll show you around. You have my number."

"I will," David said, picking up his knitting kit. "And thanks for this. I'll have the quotes to you by Thursday end of business."

"I'll be looking forward to it," she said.

He turned and started walking towards the door, then stopped beside a display of acrylic paints.

"Did you forget something?" Laura asked.

He hesitated for a moment. "I'm actually thinking of finding myself in North Powell this coming Saturday night," he said. "Will you be around?"

"I close up shop at seven on Saturdays," she said. "So yeah, I should be around."

He still looked a little nervous, as if he wasn't sure if that was a firm yes. "So . . .?"

"So meet me here at seven. I'll take you on a tour of the neighborhood."

"Okay then," he said, looking happy. "I'll see you Saturday."

"See you Saturday," Laura said.

Her positive energy became elation. It was a date.

CHAPTER 3

It was Saturday evening, six thirty. Cake Decorating for Seniors, her most popular course, was in session. But instead of huddling around cakes, her six septuagenarian students were huddled around a laptop screen.

Benita elbowed Laura. "The scene I told you about is coming up," she said.

"Shh!" said Susan. "Laura doesn't need a narrator."

"She's never seen it before," Benita said. "This is the best part."

"It's okay, really, I think I get the gist," Laura said.

"You're just going to have to trust us on this one," Susan said. "You need to see this. From the beginning. Pam, go back about one minute."

Pam scrolled the episode back sixty seconds. "Keep your big mouth shut this time," she said to Benita, "and let the girl enjoy herself."

"Really," Laura said, "it's okay—"

"Just shut up and watch." Pam hit the play button and the scene began again from the beginning.

Sam and Diane were fighting. "Are you as turned on as I am?" Sam said angrily.

"More!" Diane hollered back.

As 1982's favorite mismatched couple engaged in a passionate make-out session, Laura pulled out her phone and scrolled through the texts that she and David had been exchanging for five days. Most were short and sweet, and hard to interpret as anything but flirtatious.

> *Hi Laura, thanks again for the knitting kit.*
> *Hi David, no problem, thanks for carrying my briefcase.*
> *Anything for you, Laura.*
>
> *Hi David. 'Loved to Death in Suburbia' is on Lifetime this weekend. Care to join me? We can make oatmeal.*
> *I take back my 'Anything for you, Laura.'*
> *Fine. We'll make bran muffins.*
> *Now you're talking. Can't wait to see you again! Me too.*

All short and sweet. Until the text she received on Thursday morning. Short, yes. Sweet? Not so much.

> *Hey Laura, I sent you the three quotes by email and cc'd Carolyn. Please have a look and let me know which works best for you.*

The email had not been a pretty one. The highest quote was two hundred and eighty thousand dollars. The cheapest was one hundred and fifty, a full fifty thousand higher than her max budget.

She'd sent back an equally short, less-than-sweet reply.

> *I'll never marry you now.*

It was supposed to be a joke, but it wasn't until an hour after she sent the text that she realized David might not see it that way. He'd no doubt fought tooth and nail to convince his office that North Powell was worthy of KPS's goodwill, and she didn't want to seem ungrateful. But getting a hundred thousand dollars out of the town council had been like pulling teeth. There was no way they were going to approve a budget increase. The goodwill offering was dead in the water.

She looked at the time. 6:45. Class ended at 6:50.

"Five minutes, ladies," she said.

The grandma brigade dutifully cleaned up after themselves, and by 6:55, they were out the door and walking down Main Street towards St. Martin's Church for Saturday-night bingo and a fish fry. David would be walking through the door any minute now. That meant Laura had only a matter of minutes to brush her teeth and fix her hair and makeup. She wanted to look nice, but not so nice that it looked like she'd put in extra effort.

But just as she was considering how much makeup would seem natural, she heard a knock on the store window. David was standing outside. She waved him in.

He looked different out of the suit. He wore a tan shirt that was form-fitting enough to showcase his very nice upper body, jeans that showed off his long legs, and sneakers. His hair, so neatly combed when she met him five days ago, now looked mussed, like he had barely run his fingers through it. He still wore those sexy glasses, though.

"Hey, David," she said. "Great to see you."

"You sure about that?" he said. "I was worried you were never going to speak to me again after the quotes I sent."

"Don't be silly," she said, trying to make up for her snarky text. The professional relationship between KPS and North Powell was already over, but the personal relationship between her and David was just beginning. She didn't want the premature failure of the former to hinder the success of the latter. The fact was she had two competing needs—one, to save her beloved hometown from its plummeting economy, and two, to rescue her beloved hormones from their two-year drought. And at this particular moment, with David Harper standing before her in that form-fitting shirt, her hormones were winning the "most needy" contest. "I know you did your best for us," she said. "I wish we could have hired KPS, but there are plenty of marketing firms out there in our price range. We'll be okay."

He looked confused. "Did I miss something?"

"What do you mean?"

"I mean Carolyn signed the hundred-fifty-thousand-dollar contract and wired the retainer yesterday. As far as I know, the marketing kickoff meeting is scheduled for Monday morning."

It took her a moment to digest the news. "I'm in charge of the marketing campaign. How could I not have heard of this?"

"I don't know," David said. "I just assumed you knew."

"Where's the meeting?"

David pulled out his phone and began scrolling through his texts. When he found the one from Carolyn, he began reading it out loud.

> *Confirming that Laura will meet with you Monday 10am at 416 Main Street, Room 2. No need to cc me on further correspondences. This was Laura's thing and she's your problem, not mine.*

David looked up. "416 Main Street. I thought the town hall was at 100 Main Street?"

"It is," Laura said.

"Then where's 416?"

"You're standing in it. Room 2 is the sewing classroom and Monday is my day off. I guess that's what I get for working for free."

She could see David trying not to laugh. "You didn't actually volunteer for this, did you?"

"It's a labor of love," Laura said, shrugging. "For the town, I mean. Not Carolyn. That's just slave labor."

"You must really love this place to put up with that woman for free."

"You have no idea the things I put up with for the love of North Powell. Anyway, enough about my indentured servitude. Are you hungry?"

"I am," he said. "What's good around here?"

"Sandwiches," Laura said. "It's supposed to be a really nice night so I just went ahead and packed us a picnic. Is that okay?"

"That sounds great. I haven't been on a picnic in years."

"Hope you like mayonnaise."

"It just so happens that mayonnaise is my favorite food," David said. "Did you pack two spoons or are we going to use our fingers?"

Laura laughed, then nudged him with her elbow. "If you don't behave yourself, you're not getting any horseradish for dessert."

They walked toward the front door and, like before, he held it open for her. But this time he went a little further, placing his hand on the small of her back as she walked through. Even the light touch of his fingers was stimulating. The evening was off to a great start.

"So where are we headed?" David said.

"We can do Winter Park or we can hike to somewhere a little more private. If you're okay with climbing, I'll take you to see North Powell's largest slab of granite. This is one of the best times of the year for viewing."

"There's a granite-viewing season? That's a thing?"

"You'd be amazed at what qualifies as a 'thing' around here. Yes, there's a granite-viewing season, and it's just starting. It'll involve some steep hiking on loose rocks, so if you're not into climbing—"

"Lead the way."

"So you are into climbing?"

"No," David said. "I can't even climb the rock wall at the gym. But if anyone asks me how my date went, I want to be able to use the words 'mayonnaise' and 'granite' in the same sentence, so let's do it."

"This way," she said.

They walked to the next block and turned left onto Mulvaney.

"So," she said, hoping to hear that he had reason to come to the mountains on a regular basis, "do you have a lot of family up this way?"

"Me?" he said. "No, it's just my mother and me."

"Where's everyone else?"

"Nowhere," he said. "I'm the only child of two only children. My father died when I was eleven. So it's literally just my mother and me."

She stopped in her tracks, looking at him in near awe. "Wow," she said.

"Yeah," David said, shrugging, "it seems to surprise a lot of people."

"That's not what I meant," she said as they resumed walking. "I meant, 'Wow, this is the first time in my entire life that I've ever met someone besides myself who only has one other family member.'"

This time it was David who stopped in his tracks. "You're kidding," he said.

"I'm not," she said. "Same thing as you. My parents were only children and my father died when I was four. It's just my mom and me."

He nodded knowingly. "So people have been treating you like a helpless orphan your whole life? Giving you that look?"

"Yes," she said, knowing exactly what 'look' he was talking about. "I hate it. I started making up fake aunts and uncles when I was about six just so I wouldn't have to deal with people's pity."

They turned a corner. "So I suppose you and your mom are pretty close," David said.

"Thick as thieves. What about you?"

"For better or for worse," he said, "yeah, my mom and I are very close. You know how it is. When you only have one person in your life, you tend to cling to them pretty tightly."

"Who's the clingy one?"

"Oooh," he said, laughing, "it's her."

She gave a mental sigh of relief. He was a loyal and dutiful son, but not a mama's boy.

Time to change the subject. "This way next," she said, directing him to turn on Maple Street toward the first of the three blocks that constituted North Powell's Victorian district.

"Holy . . ." David said. "You weren't kidding when you said North Powell was quaint. Are these real kerosene streetlamps?"

"No," she said. "They're just designed to look like the real deal. But I think they have the desired effect."

"They do," he said. "I feel like I took a wrong exit off the highway and ended up in 1853. Is Rod Serling going to be making an appearance anytime soon?"

She waved him forward. "Follow me," she said. "The trail's just past that signpost up ahead."

A few yards on, they reached the foot of Octopus Trail.

"Octopus?" David said, looking at the trail map.

"It's a euphemism. The south-facing side of the mountain is rocky, so the tree roots tend to grow above the rocks in an octopus pattern. If you prefer, we can take Black Bear Gulch Trail."

"Black bear being a euphemism for . . .?"

"Black bears," she said. "The path runs past their cave."

"Octopus it is," David said. "And just remember, I'm not exactly what you'd call an experienced hiker."

"Don't worry," Laura said. "I've been hiking these mountains since I was four. I'll show you the ropes."

"It's going to be dark soon. Is this going to be safe?"

"I have a flashlight and two extra sets of batteries in my bag. And you might want to put on some mosquito repellent." She handed him her backpack. "There's a bottle in the second compartment."

"Do you always carry all this stuff with you?"

"Pretty much," she said. "A good hiker is always prepared."

"What else am I going to find in here?" he asked, digging through her bag. "A couple of grappling hooks? A hunting knife?" He looked at the "Hiking Safety" sign while coating his arms with bug spray. "'What to do if you encounter wildlife on your hike,'" he read aloud. "'Mountain lions. If you encounter a mountain lion, hold up your hands in a threatening position and growl or yell as loud as you can. If you are carrying a cell phone or flashlight, throw it at the lion to scare it away.'" He turned to Laura. "When you said there was a signpost up ahead, I wasn't actually expecting a sign telling me to challenge a mountain lion to a fistfight."

She reached into her backpack's side pocket and pulled out her hunting knife. "Here," she said, handing it over. "The mountain lions don't come out this time of night, but you can carry this if it makes you feel safer."

"I was kidding about the hunting knife, but thanks," he said, slipping it into his back pocket. "This does make me feel safer."

"Great," she said. "And like I said, it's not mountain lion season but it is rattlesnake mating season, so if you hear any rattling or hissing sounds, stay clear. And remember, you're the one holding the knife."

"Just a minute," he said, pulling her back when she took her first steps onto the trail. "Let me clarify my earlier statement. When I said I wanted to go for a hike, what I really meant was that I wanted to be alone in the woods with you. I really like you, Laura, but I'm not quite ready to die for you yet."

She put her hands on her hips, the same way she did when she was reprimanding a seven-year-old student in her beginning sewing class. "Did I scare you when I mentioned rattlesnakes?"

"No," David said. "You scared me when you mentioned mosquitos. I progressed to terrified when I saw the mountain lion sign, and now that copulating rattlesnakes have joined the club I'm thinking of just preemptively killing myself right here on the sidewalk."

"You wimping out on me, city boy?"

"I just admitted I'm afraid of mosquitos. Yes, I'm wimping out on you."

She didn't budge. If she could dirty-look a seven-year-old into confessing to pocketing a spool of pink thread, she could dirty-look a thirty-two-year-old into going for an evening hike.

David seemed amused. "That look you're giving me right now, is that a challenge?"

"Yes."

"Fine," he said, grabbing her hand. "But one of these weekends you're coming to the city and navigating the public transportation system all by yourself. We'll see how well you do on my turf."

A part of her had worried that this wasn't really a date, that David had just come to satisfy a professional curiosity about the town. But now he was holding her hand. The evening was officially romantic.

They only trekked about sixty yards before they reached a high wall of rock and dirt. "This is our first steep climb," Laura said, letting go of his hand and tightening the shoulder straps of her backpack. "Ready?"

David looked up, dismayed. "So by 'steep' you mean 'vertical'?"

"Not quite," she said. "But yes, very steep. You go first."

"I thought you were going to show me the ropes."

"I am," she said. "Use the tree roots like a ladder. I'm down here to catch you if you fall."

He gave her a cynical look.

"I'm kidding," she said. "I'll step out of the way if you fall. But I promise I'll call an ambulance afterwards."

Reluctantly, David reached up and grabbed the lowest root. With some struggle, he eventually made it up to the first of the trail's landings.

"Good job!" Laura called up. "Now, turn around and squat down so you can help me up. I'm too short to get hold of most of the roots."

On his knees, David reached down with his right arm and they grabbed each other's wrists. "Ready?" he said.

"Ready," she said.

"One, two, three." He pulled her up about four feet so she could grasp a rock on the landing. "Did I do it right?" he said.

"No," she said, gasping. "I don't have any place to put my feet."

"Oh my God," he said, gripping her under both arms and hauling her up. "Hold on, I got you."

Once he pulled her up safely, he flopped into sitting position, his legs outstretched, his eyes closed. "I thought I killed you," he panted.

"I'm fine. It gets easier from here."

He looked at her, horrified. "There's more?"

"This is just the first landing," she said. "One more to go, and then it's just a matter of following the path."

"I have a better idea," he said, his breath still labored. "Let's watch the sunset from here."

She swung her legs over the edge. Might as well give the city boy a little breather.

"Are you dangling your legs over the precipice?" he said from behind her. "That can't be safe."

"It's only a ten-foot drop," she said.

No sooner had she finished saying the word "drop" than she felt two hands grab her waist and pull her backwards. She suddenly found herself sitting between David's legs, her back pressed up against his chest.

She leaned her head back against his shoulder and closed her eyes. After a second, he rested his head upon hers.

He took her hand in his, and she felt his lips on the tops of her fingers. She closed her eyes, and instantly her imagination kicked into gear. She pictured his hands loosening their hold on her waist and reaching up to unbutton her blouse before unlatching her front-hook bra. She felt his warm hands upon her breasts, caressing, squeezing. Now he was laying her down on her back, kissing her—her forehead, her mouth, that bizarre erogenous zone just below her ear. His lips worked their way down her neck to her chest. She felt his mouth latch onto her breast, and then a tongue—

"Are you okay?" David said, sounding concerned.

She tilted her head up at him, awakened from her fantasy. "I'm fine," she said. "Why?"

"You have goose bumps. Are you cold?"

Goose bumps. All down her forearms, her hands, even her outstretched legs. She gave a slight laugh, closing her eyes and laying her head back against his shoulder. "I'm not cold," she said.

"Then why do you have goose bumps?"

"Side effect of letting my imagination run wild."

She felt him take a deep breath, and she realized that he knew what she'd been thinking. And she knew he was thinking the same thing. She was tempted to pull his face down for a kiss, but she resisted. Although she was coming off a two-year dry spell, her gut was telling her to take it slow. Yes, David was tall and handsome. But he was also smart and funny. Yes, he had a nice body. But he was also a nice person.

But more than anything else, she felt an emotional connection to him. Growing up with just one relative—and living in constant fear that you might lose the only person who loves you—was something few people could understand. She wondered if he felt the same way.

She decided to be bold and wonder out loud. "Did you ever wish it was different?" she said. "That you had a big family with grandparents and siblings and cousins and all that?"

He was quiet for a moment. "When I was a kid, sure. But now I don't think I'd change anything. You learn to value what you have, you know? Count your blessings and all that corny stuff. What about you?"

"Me?" she said, smiling. "I wish I could remember my father, but other than that, no. You meet so many people who have it all and they're still miserable. I learned early not to take anything for granted. I think I'm happier than most people because of it."

"It's nice to finally know someone else who gets it," he said, nuzzling her ear. "To meet someone who's happy and she knows it."

She immediately clapped her hands, and he laughed, pulling her in tight. She melted into his embrace; it was rare for her to feel so comfortable on a first date, and she hoped that this would be just the first of many to come.

The sun was long gone and the moon was high in the sky by the time they started heading back to Creations.

"So can I see you again next weekend?" David asked when they reached her store.

"Yes," she said. "Same time, same place?"

"Seven o'clock here," he said, then gave her a kiss on the forehead. "Thanks for a wonderful evening. I'll call you."

As she walked into her store and kicked off her shoes, she felt like a teenage girl who'd just gotten a first kiss from the boy she'd been crushing on for two years. Much too excited to go home and sleep, she decided to put her excess energy to good use and do some heavy-duty cleaning.

But as she entered the supply closet, the bell above her front door rang.

"Laura?" she heard David's voice call.

She stepped out of the closet in her bare feet to find him walking across the store toward her.

"David?" she said. "I wasn't expecting to see you back so soon. You do realize that you're a week early for our next—"

Before she could finish her sentence, he was grabbing her around the waist, lifting her off the ground, and kissing her. His lips were soft, his breath warm. She wrapped her arms around his neck as he took five steps forward and hoisted her up onto the sales counter. Through her skirt, she felt her inner thighs press against his hips.

"Please tell me I don't have to wait till next Saturday to see you again," he said, kissing her neck.

She ran a hand up his back. "When can you come back?"

"Tomorrow," he said.

"I can't," she said, dropping her forehead on his shoulder in disappointment. "There's a bake sale at church on Monday. I'll be at my mother's baking all day tomorrow."

"All day?" he said.

"All day," she said. "We'll be baking until—wait," she said. "We have a meeting on Monday, right? We'll see each other then."

"It'll just be James and Spence," he said. "I do almost all my work from the office."

"Can't you figure out some excuse for why you need to come?" she asked, hopeful.

"Not a chance," David said. "Spence already went and told everyone you were really pretty. If I finagle my way into the meeting, they're all going to know that I'm hitting on you. What are the chances you'll be able to make it to the city one night?"

"I close up shop most weeknights at six thirty, so the very earliest I could get there is seven thirty. And then I'd still have to drive all the way back."

"I barely made it through these last five days," David said, embracing her. "How am I supposed to survive a whole week without seeing you?"

"Call me," she said. "And text. And think about what you'd like to do." When he shuddered, she pulled back. "Are you okay?"

"Fine," he said. "Side effects of letting my imagination run wild."

She raised her lips to his ear. "I'm going to be up until four in the morning thinking about you."

He made a faux whimpering sound. With great reluctance, he let go of her, turned, and walked towards the door.

"I'll see you next week!" she called one last time.

"This is going to be the longest seven days of my life!" he called back as he walked out the door.

It was only their first date, but she was pretty sure she was crazy about David Harper. He was right: this was going to be the longest seven days of her life.

CHAPTER 4

If there was one thing the residents of North Powell knew how to do, it was bake.

On Monday morning, Laura and her mom sat on their wobbly plastic chairs in St. Martin's dining hall, looking over the mountains of baked goods they'd spent the last two hours arranging.

"Just looking at all this sugar is making me fat," Laura said. "Remind me what it is we're raising money for this time?"

Her mom strained to remember. "Uniforms?" she said. "For the girls' soccer team?"

"Sometimes I think that if we all just donated money instead of spending it on butter and sugar we'd be a lot richer." Laura said. "And thinner."

"Rich and thin don't build community spirit," her mom said.

"And poor and fat does?"

Her mom laughed her trademark soft laugh. Never boisterous, but always genuine.

At fifty years old, Monika Delaney remained the most beautiful woman Laura had ever seen. A slender five foot ten with high cheekbones, pale skin, and long black hair perpetually tied in a bun, she was the epitome of femininity. Despite her air of sophistication, she was in fact very down-to-earth, with a humility that never faded despite being a highly accomplished insurance professional. She was soft-spoken but firm, and unwavering in her principles. She was the perfect woman, and her only daughter had idolized her since the day she was born.

"How did someone like you manage to produce someone like me?" Laura said, pushing one of her messy red locks behind her ear.

Her mom wrapped her arm around Laura's shoulder and kissed her on the top of her head. "I had a little help from your father," she said, grasping Laura's chin gently. "You look so much like him lately."

Laura remained silent. She had turned twenty-seven in February, the same age her father was when he died. And every time her mom looked at her these days, Laura could tell she was seeing two people—her only child and her long-dead husband—in a single twenty-seven-year-old face.

"Do I remind you of him?" she asked, knowing it was a question her mom always enjoyed answering.

"More than ever," her mom said. "You were always all his. Looks. Mannerisms. Personality. He ran for town council, too, you know. Back when it was an elected and paid position."

Laura's eyes widened at this new revelation. Just when she thought there were no more stories about her dad that she'd never heard. "You never told me he was on town council."

"That's because he wasn't," her mom said, smiling. "He lost."

Her mom closed her eyes, remembering. She wasn't one for expressing her feelings, but Laura could tell she was lost in lonely thoughts.

"We should take a road trip," Laura said. "Just a few days. We haven't done that for a while."

"What did you have in mind?" her mom said. Her eyes were still closed, but her smile returned.

"What about a spa weekend? Massage? Facial? All that glam stuff we always say we're going to do and then end up going horseback riding instead?"

"I like it," her mom said, finally opening her eyes. "And let's stay somewhere nice for a change. Go for a fancy dinner. Indulge ourselves."

Laura laid her head on her mom's shoulder. "I can't wait," she said.

Her mom nudged her, pointing at the wall clock. "It's nine forty-five. Are you going to tell me about him before your ten o'clock meeting or are you just going to leave me hanging again?"

Laura was perplexed. "Tell you about who?"

"I don't know who, that's why I'm asking. All I know is that he's tall with glasses and has a cute—and I'm only saying this out loud because I'm repeating what Benita said—'tushy.'"

That could only be one person. "David," Laura said.

"Nice name."

"How does Benita know about him?"

"She said she and Pam saw a very handsome young man waiting outside your store after cake decorating class on Saturday. They could tell by the way he was looking at you that he really liked you."

"They weren't even there!"

"After they saw him go into your store, they came back and watched through the window. You two were so caught up in each other you didn't even notice them for their five whole minutes of spying."

"Good news travels fast," Laura said, a little peeved at Benita. She would have liked to have told her mom about David on her own terms. And those terms most certainly would not have included the word "tushy." "Yes, I had a date on Saturday," she admitted. "His name is David Harper and he's one of the marketing guys from KPS. And yes, he's tall and wears glasses and is very handsome. He also happens to have a personality, which is nice and smart and funny."

Her mom waited patiently. "And?"

"He has a nice tushy?"

"You know what I'm waiting to hear."

Laura stood up, slinging her backpack over one shoulder. "He's a gentleman, Mom. If we make it to a third date, I promise I'll tell you all about him. Or maybe I'll just leave my curtains up and let Benita tell you all about him." She leaned down and gave her mom a kiss on the cheek. "Heading to the meeting. Love you."

"Love you, too, princess," her mom said as Laura walked away.

When Laura walked into her shop, James and Spence were already in the sewing room in the back. James sat in the swivel chair talking on the phone and Spence was on the floor playing with the antique sewing machine.

"Bonnie," James said, "what did I just tell you . . . No, I said give Becca her doll back . . . Because you're not her boss, that's why . . . Fine, have it your way, but I saw a sign for a bake sale and I was going to bring home some brownies—"

Spence reached for the phone. "You want me to take care of that?"

"Please," a frustrated James said as he handed his cell to Spence.

"Hey, Bonnie," Spence said as he fondled the sewing machine's bobbin. "Can you do me a big favor and give Becca her doll back? . . . You can? . . . Thank you . . . Love you, too. Bye."

He returned the phone to James.

"Why do they listen to you and not me?" James said.

Spence pressed the sewing machine's foot pedal up and down with his hand. "I'm cuter."

Laura chose that moment to walk in. "Hello, gentlemen," she said. "Hope I'm not interrupting."

"Laura," James said, standing up. "I'm sorry. I didn't even hear you come in."

"I didn't know you had kids," she said. "How old are they?

"Nine, four, and six months," James said, tucking his phone back into his briefcase. "It never ends."

"No worries," she said, laying her bag on the table. She briefly considered asking why Spence had said *I love you* to James's kid, but decided to mind her own business.

James nodded toward the sewing machine. "I don't believe we mentioned this in our first meeting, but part of David's job is to keep Spence and me in line. As you can see, Spence is taking this opportunity to demonstrate exactly why that is. Spence, care to join the meeting?"

When Spence rose to his feet, Laura realized he was about four or five inches taller than she remembered, easily six foot two.

"Were you this tall last week?" she asked him.

"Was I here last week?"

"Do you see what I have to deal with?" James said.

Spence sat down at the table, found a pencil and started twirling it between his fingers.

"So," James began, "after looking at the notes you sent, we had a few thoughts that we'd like to run by you."

"Absolutely," Laura said, taking her seat. She looked over at Spence to see if he had anything to add, but he was busy looking at the ceiling fan.

James continued. "For the last couple of winters it looks like you've mostly advertised in *Skier's World*, at Skivacation.com, and at Wintersports.com, correct?"

"Correct."

"So, basically, you're advertising to skiers but you don't have any ski slopes. Furthermore, you're advertising in venues that cater to the twenty-one-to-thirty-year-old demographic even though you don't have a liquor store. Bainbridge has eleven night clubs. Haven has fourteen bars. Haven also has the hot springs and Bainbridge is building an alpine slide they expect to have completed by the end of October."

"If you're trying to make me feel better," she said, "it's not working."

James leaned back in his chair. "My point is that when you advertise in places like *Skier's World*, you're only advertising your deficiencies. What you need to do is stop telling the world what you don't have, and start showing off what you do."

"Okay," she said, starting to see James's point. "I think I follow."

"So," he continued, "what are North Powell's strengths?"

"Well," she began, "I'd say our biggest strength is our way of life. Except for the mayor everyone's really nice. Everyone knows everyone else. And there's a never-ending supply of baked goods."

"I mean from a tourist's perspective," James said.

Laura thought about it for a minute. "From a tourist's perspective? I guess our biggest draw is just the way the town looks. You can see for yourself how beautiful Main Street is, and our Victorians are the oldest in the state. And we have some of the best hiking and horseback riding trails around. And every spring we sponsor a butterfly pavilion that I'm sure your kids would love." She sighed. "But let's be real. None of that can compete with Bainbridge or Haven."

"You're right," James said, "it can't."

Despite the fact that she knew he was right, she took offense. But she tried to maintain a calm and professional demeanor. "James," she said, "I really appreciate KPS's willingness to work for such a discounted rate. But a hundred and fifty thousand dollars is *a lot* of money for us, and if you're telling me that we're never going to be able to compete with Haven and Bainbridge, it might be better for us to cut our losses right now."

"I'm not saying you can't compete. I'm saying you shouldn't try to—"

"The roof on the high school gym is about to collapse and we could use that money—"

"What I meant is that Haven and North Powell are apples and oranges—"

"We've been filling the potholes with sand, James. *Sand.* The neighborhood cats are using them as communal litter boxes and last week an eight-year-old almost got run over trying to build a castle in the middle of Selwyn Street."

From the left side of the table, Spence struggled to stifle a laugh.

"Most people don't think an eight-year-old almost getting run over is funny, Spence," James said.

"It was kind of funny, actually," Laura said in Spence's defense. "He was using cat poop as balustrades. There's a picture of it on the town website if you want to check it out."

It took Spence a beat to regain his composure, but when he did, he turned his attention to James. "Do you mind if I have a word alone with Laura? Five minutes?"

Well, this was an unexpected development.

"Um, yeah, I guess," James said. "Laura, do you mind if I run across the street for a coffee?"

"No, go ahead."

"Can I get you anything?"

"Just ask Kayla for my regular."

"Will do. Spence?"

"Just ask Kayla for my regular," he echoed.

James gave an exasperated sigh and grabbed his wallet from his briefcase. "Be back in five."

James departed, closing the door behind him.

Spence looked at Laura from across the table, actually making eye contact.

"Hey, Laura," he said.

"Hey, Spence," she said. She shifted in her seat, suddenly feeling a little uncomfortable.

"I just wanted to tell you not to listen to anything James says."

"You think he's wrong?" she said.

"James? No, he's the smartest guy I know. He's right about everything. But listening to all this technical stuff is giving you a heart attack, so stop listening."

"I have to listen," she said, feeling panic build. "This whole marketing campaign was my idea and if it doesn't work, that's it, every store in town is going to be out of business in three years' time. I have to know what's going on."

"It's one thing to know what's going on and it's another thing to worry about it," Spence said. "You can drive yourself nuts trying to understand what David and James are doing, or you can take the easy way out and trust them. That's what I do. Which doesn't change the fact that every time I'm stuck in one of these meetings I want to kill myself."

Laura sighed. "I feel you there."

"So stop listening. I stopped listening years ago, and I'm twice as effective at my job than I used to be. And after today, you'll hardly be seeing James or David anyway."

"I won't?"

"Didn't you hear the good news?" Spence said. "After this meeting, you're all mine."

Okay, now she was totally confused. "I'm all yours?"

"I'm the creative director and this is where the creative process begins. That means from this point forward, you belong to me, and your creative director is telling you to stop worrying. The point of my existence for the next six months is to take care of you." He leaned back in his chair again as the bell on her front door jingled, signaling James's return from the coffee shop. "I promise I won't let you down."

She found herself staring at Spence in a weird combination of immense appreciation and complete disbelief. "Do you always do this?" she asked him. "Kick your coworkers out of the room to tell your clients to not listen to anything they say?"

"No," he said. "This is the first time."

"And what makes me so special?"

He didn't answer, just gave her a wink as James walked back into the room.

"Tea with lemon," he said, handing Laura a cup. "So what did Spence have to say that was such a big secret?"

"He was professing his love for me," Laura said, "but I had to break his heart." She was going to give Spence a wink back, but he was back to analyzing the ceiling fan. "Just kidding," she said to James. "He said you're very smart and I should stop arguing and just trust you. I've decided to take his word for it."

James looked nonplussed. "Really?" he said, still on the lookout for a prank. "You trust me. Just like that?"

"Just like that."

James looked at Spence. "You're so freakin' weird, man."

"Thank you."

James looked at Laura. "Yes, he's always like this. My advice is to try to get used to it because you're going to be seeing a lot of him after today."

"So I heard."

Sliding back into his seat, James pulled his laptop out of his bag. "Well, since we're suddenly all on the same page, I'm going to log on and show you some of the venues we're thinking of advertising in." He turned his laptop around so Laura could see the screen. "What we want to do is target middle-class families with young children. North Powell has a very wholesome appeal, which is something that Haven and Bainbridge absolutely don't have." He clicked. "This website is called Familyfun.com, and—"

Just then, James's phone rang. He answered the call and put it on speaker. "Hey, David," he said. "You're on speaker. We're all here."

Laura felt a thrill just hearing David's name spoken out loud. But she was careful to maintain her poker face. If it was against the rules for David to accept a spool of yarn from a client, it was a safe bet that making out with her on her sales counter was also a big no-no.

"Hey, James," David said. "Is Laura there?"

"I'm here," Laura said.

"Hi, Laura. Nice to hear your voice again."

"Yours too, David."

David said nothing to Spence, and Spence said nothing back.

"So," David continued, "I'm just checking in to see how the meeting's going."

"It's going very well," James said. "We've decided that we're going to stop marketing to skiing and winter-sports enthusiasts and focus instead on the family and religious markets. They're the more appropriate target and also the most economically feasible when it comes to advertising venues."

"Great," David said. "Laura, when we last spoke you told me you want to do whatever you can on your end to keep costs down, correct?"

"Absolutely."

"In that case, James, what should Laura be doing while you're looking into advertising opportunities?"

"Well, I think it's really important to get the whole town on board with this, especially the B and B and shop owners. The more work they do themselves, the more money we can allocate to advertising. So Laura needs to let everyone in town know that the marketing campaign has started and that their own efforts in promoting the town are every bit as important as ours."

"I agree," David said. "Spence?"

"Yeah?"

"What do you think?"

"About what?"

"Laura."

"She's okay, I guess. I don't really know her that well yet."

There was a pause on David's end. "I meant what do you think she should be doing?"

"It's supposed to be her day off," Spence said. "I guess she could read a book or something, but it's not really any of my business."

In a barely audible voice, David muttered, "Markham. Christ. Why do I even bother?" Then, in a normal tone, "James, what are next steps?"

"We're wrapping up here for today and then Spence and I are heading back to the office to start our research. But before we begin to develop a campaign, we need to decide exactly what it is about North Powell we're going to advertise, so Spence and Laura are going to start meeting here on Mondays to help familiarize him with the town and discern—"

Laura made an "X" sign with her fingers while mouthing, *Monday's my day off.*

James swiveled his chair around so that he was facing the wall. "Monday is Laura's day off, but she's agreed to sacrifice it and meet with Spence every Monday for the next several weeks to make sure the campaign is a success. We've already ascertained that they have a butterfly pavilion every spring. That alone should be marketable, not just to families but also to nature enthusiasts."

"Wow, that does sound like a lot of progress. Great job, guys."

"Thanks, David," Laura and James said.

"And Laura, I'll give you a call later in the week to check in."

"Looking forward to it, David."

The call, and the meeting, concluded.

Spence looked at Laura. "Next Monday, same time and place?"

"Sounds good to me."

James stood, nodding toward Spence. "He has a degree in mechanical engineering and he's pretty smart if you can get him to focus," he said. "But just to be safe, you might want to start next week's meeting by slipping him some ADHD medication. And keep him away from that antique sewing machine. He'll take the whole thing apart just so he can put it back together."

The two men began gathering up their things. When they were all packed up, Laura walked them to the front door.

"Well, Laura," James said, "I think we're off to a good start. Thanks for a great meeting."

"Thank you, James. Talk to you soon. Bye, Spence."

"Bye, Laura," Spence said. "Thanks in advance for the Adderall."

She watched them walk away, feeling like she knew them both a little better now. James was a little more easygoing than he'd seemed last week, and Spence was a little more . . . whatever. She couldn't pinpoint an exact word for it. But he'd be back in a week. She'd find out for herself soon enough.

CHAPTER 5

On Saturday, Laura shoved her cake decorating students out the front door and pointed them toward St. Martin's, though she doubted any of them would be eating any fish tonight. Class had only been in session for five minutes before they'd succumbed to the power of Ted Danson. By 6:15, Laura had abandoned all hope and just given them each a tub of chocolate frosting and a plastic spoon.

Her heart started racing when she saw David's car pull into a space across the street. She hadn't seen him since last Saturday night, and it had been a long and lonely week. She stepped into the display window and immediately began drawing the shades, lest David's arrival give anyone in town the opportunity to use the word "fanny," or even worse, "keister."

She was pulling down the last shade when the bell rang. "Hey, David," she said. "How was the drive up?"

"Fine," he said. "How did class go?"

"Not so great," she said, walking over to him. "Sam and Diane are getting really tired of Coach tagging along on their dates."

She expected some kind of clever retort, having no doubt that David's mother had subjected him to all eleven seasons of *Cheers*, but he just pulled her in and wrapped his arms around her. "And at last my weekend begins," he said. "It's been a very, very long week."

She closed her eyes as she laid her head on his chest. "Busy?" she whispered.

"No more than usual," he said. "But I had a date with this really great girl last Saturday and I had to wait seven whole days to see her again. It was torture."

He leaned in for a kiss, and she melted at the touch of his lips upon hers. He was a good kisser. And he was right. It had been a long, long week.

At last, they separated. "I thought maybe we could go to my house and order in tonight," she said.

"Sounds perfect," he said. "But I was going to take you out for a nice dinner, so at the very least let me buy."

"You're the one who drove in all the way from the city," she said. "Let me."

"You made us mayonnaise sandwiches last Saturday—"

"Which we never ate—"

"I'm paying," he insisted. "It's my way of saying thank you for making me so stupidly happy that I haven't gotten anything done for an entire week."

She tried to contain her excitement. He was thinking of her to the point of distraction and was "stupidly happy" about it. "Let's head back to my place," she said.

Less than ten minutes later, they arrived at her tiny bungalow. They had barely crossed the threshold when Laura turned to him. There was a business matter she needed to get out of the way before their date began in earnest. "So," she said, "what's the deal with Spence Markham?"

David rolled his eyes. "Is that ever a loaded question," he said.

"That bad?" she said.

"No, no," David conceded as they walked into the kitchen. "He's a good guy. He and I don't always see eye to eye, but he's very good at his job." He picked her up by the hips and sat her on the end of the island. "At any rate, he'd better be. He certainly gets paid enough for it. Why do you ask?"

"I don't know," she said as she twined her fingers behind his neck. "I remember at the first meeting, I thought he looked like someone who had wandered into the meeting by accident while he was sleepwalking."

"Oh my God," David said, raising his hands toward the ceiling as if to say "Hallelujah!"

"What did I say?" Laura said, surprised at his extreme reaction.

"The exact words I've been looking for for ten years," he said, placing his hands back on her waist. "'A sleepwalker who wandered into the meeting by accident.' You've captured his corporate persona perfectly. Please tell me I can use that in conversation."

"No!" she said. "You can never ever repeat that. And besides, what I was going to say is that he seemed completely different on Monday than our first meeting."

"Like how?"

"Like . . . I don't know, really. I can't find a word for it."

"Weird," David said. "The word you're looking for is weird."

"Yeah, weird about covers it. But smart, too. Right?"

"Yeah, he's smart. He's a weird, smart, overpaid pain in my ass." David was smiling, but Laura detected a hint of genuine resentment in his voice.

She decided to change the subject. "I believe you said you were hungry. What are you in the mood for?"

"I haven't had a girlfriend in two years, so I think you already know the answer to that question. But if my first choice isn't available, I'll settle for food."

She raised an eyebrow at him. "Do you want to look at a menu or not?"

"You come with a menu?" he said. "Hell yeah, I want to see it. Is it à la carte?"

She tried not to laugh. And failed. "Hmm. What was that you were saying about Spence Markham being weird?"

"I was talking about work weird," he said, tightening his grip around her waist. "This is pretty-girl-on-a-kitchen-counter weird. My weird is way better than his."

"You," she said, pulling him toward her by his shirt collar, "are way goofier than you look."

She kissed him, and a satisfied *mmm* sound came from his throat as she wrapped her legs around his waist. When he ran his hands just high enough under her skirt to caress her bare thighs, she tightened the grip of her legs. This time there was no playfulness, no interruptions. And also no dinner.

Another lovely Saturday evening was in progress.

CHAPTER 6

The following Monday morning, Laura waited in the sewing room for Spence's arrival. She was uncharacteristically nervous. Thanks to years of teaching classes, she'd learned how to make conversation with anyone. But Spence? She couldn't even think of how to initiate one. She had spent the entire morning thinking about it, and so far all she had come up with was "Hi."

"Hi."

She jumped. There was Spence, standing about two feet behind her. "Oh my God, you scared me."

"Sorry," he said, handing her a paper cup. "I didn't mean to come in so quietly. Tea with lemon, right?"

"I'm impressed," she said. "So you *were* paying attention during last week's meeting."

"Only to the important things like beverages. The marketing stuff is kind of a blur."

His phone rang. He pulled it out and looked at the caller ID. "Sorry, I have to take this. I'll make it quick."

"No hurry," she said.

He stepped out of the sewing room. She could hear him mumbling something about a two-million-dollar lobby renovation and the words "waste of money if you ask me." A few moments later he came back inside. "Sorry," he said, again. "Mondays."

"No problem," she said. And then, a little more awkwardly, "I've got to tell you, I don't really understand what it is we're supposed to be doing today."

"I believe you're supposed to be helping me familiarize myself with the town so I can determine its most marketable attributes and develop an economically feasible game plan."

Laura laughed at his impression of James. "Well," she said, "I don't think spending any more time sitting in my sewing room is going to help you familiarize yourself with anything other than quilting fabric. It's a gorgeous day. Do you feel like wandering?"

"I love wandering," Spence said.

They stepped outside into the sun. "There's a lot I can show you," she said, "but one of the things we'd really like to promote is our B and Bs. This way."

She gestured to him to follow her toward Mulvaney Street, where they walked one block in to stop at the corner of Maple.

"So these three blocks, Maple, Oak, and Chestnut, are the main drag for B and Bs. We have sixteen in total," she said.

Spence stared down Maple Street, looking a little awestruck. "This is gorgeous," he said. "I had no idea there was a town anywhere in the state that looked like this. Do you think we could tour a couple of them?" he asked.

"Absolutely. Any one in particular catch your eye?"

He didn't hesitate. "That one," he said, pointing to the most decrepit house on the street, a large blue Victorian with a dilapidated façade, a sagging porch and a tree branch growing through one of the upstairs windows.

She looked down, smiling to herself. "Good choice," she said.

A short minute later they were walking up the front steps.

"Welcome to Powell House," she said as she unlocked the front door.

"Do you have the keys to every house in town?" Spence said as Laura struggled to push the heavy wooden door open.

"No," Laura said. "Just this one. This was the first house built and the owner was the last surviving Powell. She died in January and left the house and her entire life savings to the town."

"That was generous," he said.

"It was," Laura said. "But her entire savings was only a hundred thousand dollars."

"*Only* a hundred thousand dollars?"

"Let me elaborate," Laura said. "I agreed to allocate forty thousand to the marketing campaign. The rest I set aside for repairs and renovations. New plumbing. New HVAC. And I'm also obviously going to have to invest in a new front door," she said, still struggling to get it open. "Can you help me with this?"

He grabbed the doorknob, but instead of pushing forward, pulled up. The door opened right away.

He squatted down and motioned to Laura to follow suit. "The bottom of the door is warped," he explained, running his fingertips along the splintered bottom rim. "Probably from melting snow on the porch. You don't have to replace it, you just have to shave an inch off the bottom."

"Thanks for the advice," she said, relieved. "I'll try to get to that this weekend."

His phone rang again, and once again he looked at the caller ID. "I'm sorry," he said. "I'll try to make this quick."

"Take your time," she said.

As he talked to a coworker about something called "Harbinger," he walked into the library and tried to open one of the windows. It was painted shut.

How old are these? he mouthed.

One hundred and forty, she mouthed back. *Give or take.*

"Sounds good," he said aloud. "See you at the meeting tomorrow." He stuck his phone in his back pocket. "So how did you end up in charge of Powell House?"

"The house and property itself were left to the town, but Mrs. Powell made the town treasurer—me, as it turns out—the trustee. So I don't own anything, but I'm in charge of the funds and I have the final call on all decisions."

"Don't you have enough on your plate?" he said as he toyed with one of the bricks on the fireplace's crumbling façade.

"I don't mind," she said, walking over to the built-in bookcase she'd spent all day yesterday sanding. She ran her fingertips along the now-smooth surface of one of the empty shelves. "In a masochistic kind of way, I really enjoy it. Something about being alone here at night, working with my hands, taking something old and ugly and making it new and beautiful again. It's very peaceful."

She looked over to him, only to find him already looking at her. "I'm sorry," she said. "You asked me a simple yes or no question and I turned it into a poetry slam. The short answer is yes, I already have enough on my plate."

He continued his tour while composing a text. "I take it these are the original floors?" he said, walking back into the entryway.

"All the floors except those in the bathroom and kitchen are original," she said.

"Do you mind if I take some pictures?" he said. "My dad's a master carpenter. He does almost all his work renovating old houses. He'll know just by looking at the pictures what can be repaired and what needs to be replaced."

"Sure," she said. "Take as many pictures as you want. I can use all the help I can get."

He stopped at the foot of the well-worn staircase. "Do you mind if I check out the upstairs?"

"Be my guest," Laura said. "Just make sure to walk on the left side of the steps. And don't use the handrail. And also there's a hole at the top. Try not to step in it."

He gave her an amused glance. "Anything else I should know before I head up?"

"Don't open the last door on the right. That's where I keep the bodies."

"Noted."

Laura followed Spence up to the second floor, then to the largest bedroom in the house. She watched from the doorway as he sat down on the bed. The only other piece of furniture was an antique mirror. The windows were so dirty you couldn't see out of them.

Spence hit the mattress lightly with the palm of his hand. A cloud of dust floated upward.

"So you like Powell House?" Laura said.

"It's great. Hard to find houses with this kind of character these days," he said. "What are you planning to do with it after you're done renovating?"

"There's been talk of turning it into a museum. Or possibly a library. Or a combination of both."

"Sounds like an expensive project," he said. "I'm surprised the town's willing to put up that kind of money." He looked at Laura, waiting for an explanation on how the hell the town was going to be able to afford the cost of building a museum *and* library when it could barely afford sand for its potholes.

She sat down beside him on the bed. After a moment of hesitation, she confessed. "So when I say there's been talk, what I mean is that I kind of talk to the house when I'm here alone working. I've never actually mentioned the whole library and museum thing to a corporeal being."

He looked up at a large water stain on the ceiling and smiled. "We're going to make a good team," he said. He took a picture of the stain. "So what does everyone else in town want to do with the house?"

"It's still under discussion, but the word 'arson' gets thrown around a lot."

He dropped his head, laughing. "Well, for what it's worth, I think turning it into a museum and/or library is a great idea."

His phone rang. She sneaked a look at the caller ID. It was David.

"Do you need to take that?" she said.

"No," he said, hitting the decline button. "Can I see the rest of the rooms?"

"Follow me," she said, pretending she didn't notice that David's was the one call he'd ignored. "I'll show you something I think you'll really like."

He followed her down the hall to a small, dark room.

"Is somebody squatting here?" Spence asked, toeing the twin mattress on the floor.

"Just me," she said. "I come here a lot after I close the shop. I kept falling asleep on the floor, so I finally just brought my old mattress from my mom's house. But that's not what I wanted to show you. There's a stepstool in the corner. Can you give it to me?"

He reached over for the stepstool. "Where do you want it?"

"Up against the wall," she said, moving out of the way as he unfolded it.

She climbed up to the third step. He climbed to the second step, so that he was standing directly behind her, his front side separated from her backside by no more than a few inches.

"What am I supposed to be seeing?" he asked.

She held her flashlight up so that it illuminated some writing on the wall behind the peeling wallpaper. Spence squinted as he tried to decipher the ancient handwriting. "Does that say Grover Cleveland?" he asked, his interest piqued.

"Keep reading," she said.

"I'll try." He leaned in closer. "'Grover Cleveland is a . . .'" He pulled down the corner of the wallpaper so he could read the rest. "'Grover Cleveland is a flapdoodle.'" He paused for a moment, as if he wasn't sure he was reading it right. "A flapdoodle? What's that, some ancient political party like the Whigs?"

"I looked it up on Wikipedia," Laura said. "Evidently it's late-eighteen-hundreds slang for a man who was sexually impotent."

Behind her, Spence stepped off the stool. When she turned around, he was bent perpendicular at the waist with his hands on his knees. He was doing that thing where you're laughing so hard you're not even making any noise.

"Spence?" she said. "Are you okay?"

He stood up straight, still laughing. "This is the first time I've ever found Grover Cleveland to be even remotely interesting. Yeah, I'm fine."

"Are you crying?" she said.

"No," he said as he wiped what appeared to be a laughter-induced tear from his eye. "Okay, maybe just a little." He took a few deep breaths before composing himself. "Alright, I'm back. Mind if I check out the other rooms?"

"Be my guest."

He took his time wandering in and out of rooms, exploring the vast second floor in all its dirty, musty, cobwebby glory.

At last he completed his self-guided tour and joined her back in the hallway.

"I can see you have a personal attachment to this house," he said, crossing his arms over his chest, "so I feel guilty for saying this, but wouldn't you make a lot more money for the town if you just sold it?"

"I've thought about it, trust me. But I'm afraid the buyer will tear it down and build something that isn't architecturally sympathetic to the rest of the neighborhood."

"How do you mean?"

"I mean North Powell's greatest strength as a tourist town is that it looks like something straight out of *A Tale of Two Cities*. If someone tears down Powell House and builds some new age monstrosity in its place, it will ruin the character and charm of the entire Victorian district. And character and charm are all we have left."

He nodded, suddenly looking very introspective.

"What?" she said.

"Can we go back outside? Look around the neighborhood a little more?"

"Sure," she said.

For the next fifteen minutes, they wandered up and down the streets of the Victorian district in silence. Spence appeared to be lost in thought, and she didn't want to interrupt KPS's "best idea guy" while his mental cogs were spinning.

They wrapped up their tour exactly where they started it, on the front steps of Powell House.

"The cobblestones and the streetlamps," he said, "are they original?"

"The cobblestones are. The streetlamps were installed in the eighties, back when the town still had money."

He crossed his arms in front of his chest again, slowly tapping his right elbow with his fingertips. "Have you ever offered anything period-centric to tourists? Horse-drawn carriages? That sort of thing?"

"We haven't," she said. "But I like the idea. And I think tourists would love it."

He tapped his elbow some more. "So you've read a lot of Charles Dickens?" he asked, referring to her comment about North Powell looking like a scene out of *A Tale of Two Cities.*

"Every word," she said. "I wrote my senior thesis on him."

He nodded, thinking. "What do you think about a Dickens-themed festival?" he said.

"How do you mean?"

"We're specifically focusing on holiday tourism, right? I don't think any author evokes Christmas like Charles Dickens, and I'm pretty sure no town in this state evokes Dickens like North Powell. So you have a Dickens Festival at the start of the holiday shopping season. You can invite tourists to dress up like their favorite Dickensian character. Have a Dickens reading at the church. The restaurants can serve period food. And I'd say any one of the houses on this street could pass for Santa's workshop. I'm just thinking off the top of my head here, but—"

"But nothing, Spence," she said, growing excited. "That's a great idea!"

"You like it?"

"I love it," she said. "Do you think we could get something like that all planned out by December?"

"We'd have to start right away," he said. "But yeah, I think we could swing it." He caught the way she was looking at him. "What?" he said.

"He was right," she said.

"Who was?"

"David. He said you're a lot smarter than you look."

"He said that? Out loud to a client?"

"I think he meant it as a compliment."

"I guess it's better than 'He's not as stupid as he looks.' That's what he says to most people."

"Well, I'm not sure I believe you," she said. "But I have noticed that you and David don't always seem to be on the same page."

"Yeah," Spence said, shrugging, "he likes to give me a hard time."

"How do you mean?"

"He's okay outside the office, but in terms of business he's very buttoned-down and old-school. It's not like we hate each other or anything—I've learned to respect him and he's learned to tolerate me. And for some twisted reason, we make a good team, so we're stuck with each other until he finally gets around to murdering me."

They sat down on the front steps of Powell House.

"Do you mind if I make a personal observation?" Laura said.

Spence winced. "Every time someone says that to me at work they're about to politely criticize my sneakers."

"I have absolutely no opinion on your sneakers," Laura said, looking down at his feet. "I take it back, they're awful. But that's not what I was going to say. What I was going to say is that you are a *completely* different person one-on-one than you are in a group setting."

"I suppose," he said, shrugging. "I just like to let James and David do the talking."

"So next time we have a meeting with all four of us, are you actually going to speak and make eye contact or are you going to be all quiet and weird again?"

He smiled just a little. "I'm going to be all quiet and weird again," he said. "If that's okay with you?"

"Tell you what," she said. "I won't tell anyone that you're secretly nice and normal and even somewhat pleasant if you don't tell anyone that I'm potentially squandering sixty thousand dollars of the town's money renovating a house that might never be legally inhabitable."

"I'll keep your secret if you keep mine," Spence said, extending his hand for a shake. "Deal?"

They shook on it. "Deal."

CHAPTER 7

"Have I told you yet how much I missed you this past week?" David said, stroking her hair as they lay on the sofa, her head snuggled against his chest.

They'd been seeing each other for six weeks now, and it hadn't taken long for the "Saturday only" schedule to morph into dates on Monday and Wednesday evenings, then an overnight on Friday. And on the days they couldn't meet in person, they always facetimed before bed. But David had had a killer schedule this week, and so for the first time in a month, they hadn't seen each other since the previous Saturday.

"You told me," she whispered. "But feel free to tell me again."

"I missed you like crazy," he said. "No more going six days in a row without seeing each other. My heart can't take it."

The urge to tell him she loved him was hitting her about ten times a week these days. But every time the urge hit, she suppressed it. If he didn't reciprocate, she'd curl up and die. So, as always, she remained silent.

"Have you ever thought about Bainbridge?" he continued. "I know it's not your favorite place in the world, but if you lived there, we could probably see each other in person every day, even if we only met at a halfway point. And you'd only have to commute forty minutes to the shop."

She knew that most people would be scared off by such topics of conversation after only six weeks of dating. But David was not most people, and neither was she. It harkened back to that conversation they'd had on their very first date, about how having very little teaches you to count your blessings. He wanted to be closer to her because she was something he valued. And she wanted to be closer to him because she didn't take him for granted. They knew what they had in each other.

But what he was suggesting was impossible, and not just because a one-room condo above a laundromat in Bainbridge cost about ten million dollars. "I can't leave my mother, David," she said. "I'm all she has. She's all I have."

He pulled her in tight, laying a kiss on her forehead. "You have me," he said.

There it was again, on the tip of her tongue, desperate to escape her lips. *I love you, David.*

"So you've told me all about your mom," she said instead. "What about your dad? Was he a good father?"

"My father?" David said. "The best. Smartest guy I ever knew. Funny as hell. And he had a huge heart. You would have liked him." He gave her a squeeze. "And he would have loved you."

She lifted her head. She had a long history of seeking fatherly approval from any and all available sources, and she wasn't about to miss an opportunity. "Do you really think so?"

"Of course I do." He brushed a stray curl from her face. "What's there not to love?"

She laid her head back down on his shoulder, smiling just a little at the sound of his voice using the word love.

"Do you ever visit him?" she asked. "His grave, I mean?"

"He was cremated."

"Oh. Where was he scattered?"

"No one's sure," David said. "When my mom picked up his ashes from the crematorium, she accidently left the urn on the roof of the car. We think he's spending eternity somewhere on the westbound I-70 corridor. Hopefully near the Purina plant. Father did so love his cat food."

She cracked up. He'd made her laugh the very first time they met, and he'd been making her laugh ever since. "I don't know if I ever told you this, but your sense of humor is the first thing that attracted me to you," she admitted. "But for real. Where was he scattered?"

David met her glance. He wasn't smiling.

"Oh, my God," she said, horrified. "I'm so sorry, I thought you were kidding."

"I was kidding about him loving cat food. The rest is unfortunately true."

She shut her mouth, trying to focus her mind on all things awful. Poverty. Hunger. Oppression.

"You're still laughing."

"I'm sorry," she said. "I'm trying to get the mental image out of my head."

"It's okay," he said, laughing along with her. "My father had a warped sense of humor. I'm pretty sure it was an ending he would have appreciated."

He pulled her up on top of him. "Do you enjoy this?" he said, tugging at the sides of her panties through the fabric of her silky nightie. "Walking into the room dressed like that, showing off those gorgeous curves and then not letting me see what's underneath?"

She sat herself upright so that her thighs straddled his hips. She could feel his erection pressing up between her legs, and couldn't help but move back and forth a little. "If I'm not mistaken," she said, "you were the one who came into the kitchen after work, handed me this lovely outfit, and said, 'Here, I bought you something to cook dinner in.'"

"I know," he said as he pressed his hips upward. "But when I bought it I was just thinking about how good it would look on you. But now that you're wearing it, all I can think of is how good it would look off you."

He stopped moving. His demeanor was suddenly serious.

"What?" she said.

He seemed to be weighing his next words carefully. "I know you're old-fashioned," he began, cautious. "And I'm fine with taking things slow." He paused, and she expected there was a "but" coming.

"But?" she asked.

"But as you can clearly see—and feel," he said, gesturing toward their joined hips, "I'm obviously ready whenever you are."

She remained silent.

"I've actually been in a perpetual state of obvious readiness since the moment we met," he continued. "It's getting kind of embarrassing. Especially during the weekly finance meetings."

She laughed. She didn't actually believe he got "obvious" erections during finance meetings, but she understood what he meant by "perpetual state of readiness." She wanted him constantly. She fell asleep every night thinking of making love to him. She'd started setting her alarm a half hour early so that she'd have extra time to lounge in bed daydreaming about him before work. And she couldn't even count how many times in a single day she imagined them naked in a bed together.

And despite all that, she wanted to wait.

"It's not about me being old-fashioned," she said, her fingers in his hair. "And trust me, once you get me naked, old-fashioned is about the last thing I am. But that's not what the waiting is about."

"It's not?" he said. "Then what's it about?"

"You, I guess."

He raised an eyebrow. "I'm the reason we're not having sex? That really doesn't sound like me."

"What I mean is . . ." She paused, searching for the right words. "I think what I mean is that I'm having such a good time falling in love with you that I just want to drag it out and enjoy it as long as I can." She leaned down and kissed his nose. "I love daydreaming about you. I love counting down the minutes until I can see you again, and feel you again, and touch you again." She moved her mouth to his ear. "I love lying awake at night touching my breasts and wishing it was your hands on me. And most of all, I like lying naked in bed with no covers on—"

Ping.

It was her text tone.

She reached over his head to the end table for her phone, but his hand reached back and pushed hers away. "We're in the middle of something very important here. Whatever it is, it can wait."

"It might be my mom," she said. "She had a hundred-degree fever this afternoon and I just want to make sure she doesn't need me."

He reached back for the phone and handed it to her.

She read the text.

"How is she?" David asked.

"It's not her. It's Spence."

"*Spence?*"

"Yeah."

"Six hours ago this guy was complaining about how he never has any time off and now he's sending you work emails at ten o'clock on a Friday night?"

"It's not about work," she said, still reading. "It's about Powell House."

"That house that was left to the town?"

"Yeah," she said, handing him the phone. "Look."

hey laura sorry to bug you outside of work but I've been thinking about what you were saying about how expensive it's going to be to renovate Powell House and how you were worried about it being torn down and I don't know why I didn't think of this earlier but have you ever thought about trying to get it landmarked if it's a landmark no one can tear it down here's a link if you want to check it out spence

"Didn't this guy take tenth-grade English?" David said. "Didn't anyone ever teach him the danger of run-on sentences?"

"It never even occurred to me to try to have Powell House landmarked," she said, rereading the text. "But that's a really good idea, right?"

David laid the phone face-down on the end table. "It's a great idea. Can we get back to my bedtime story now?"

"Sorry," she said, smiling at his eagerness. "Where were we?"

"You were naked on a bed," he said. "And feel free to elaborate on how old-fashioned you aren't once I get you naked. I was really enjoying that part."

She laid her body back on top of his. "I love lying naked on the bed with no covers on," she said, kissing his neck. "And imagining you crawling on top of me and feeling your body on top of mine." She ran her hands up the sides of his torso and up to his chest. "I love imagining that moment when I feel you big and hard inside of me for the first time—"

Ping.

"Oh my God, what now, a link to an asbestos remediation manual?"

"Can you just check and make sure it's not my mom?"

He picked up the phone and read aloud. "'Also if it's a landmark you might be able to get a grant to restore/renovate it.'"

She sat upright again. "A grant?" she said. "As in free money?"

"I believe that's how a grant works," he said, fiddling with her phone.

"What are you doing?"

"I'm giving your mom a unique text tone," David said, followed by the sound of cooing doves. "That way you'll always know when it's her."

He kept fiddling.

"Now what are you doing?"

"I'm changing Spence's text tone."

The next sound she heard was the opening notes of the theme song to *The Shining*.

"Very funny," she said. "You know I'm changing that back as soon as you leave tomorrow."

"Do whatever you want when I leave," he said. "But I wait all week for my Friday nights with you. Is there anything wrong with me wanting to have you all to myself?"

She leaned down, pressing her forehead against his. "What did I ever do to deserve a guy like you?"

He rubbed his nose against hers. "Do you want to know what the best decision I ever made was?"

"What?" she said.

"Driving to North Powell in separate cars the day of our first meeting and getting that extra fifteen minutes alone with you. I know it's only been six weeks, but now that you're a part of my life, I can't imagine life without you."

Once again resisting the urge to say *I love you*, she closed her eyes. "I never told you the ending to your bedtime story," she whispered.

"I'm all ears," he whispered back.

She sat back up so she could get a better look at him. His eyes were closed and his glasses sat crooked over his nose. His hair was a mess and he needed a shave. He had never been sexier.

"When I said the reason I wanted to take it slow was you," she said, running her fingertips down the side of his face, "I think what I meant was that you're kind of like a really great mystery novel. I can't wait to get to the big reveal at the end, but at the same time I want the mystery to last as long as possible because I'm enjoying the story so much."

He opened his eyes, and his expression softened.

"For all I know," she continued, "this is just the first six weeks of the next fifty years of our lives. Someday we might know each other better than we know ourselves, right? So why not enjoy the mystery for as long as we can?"

He did not respond, and she had a moment of panic. She hadn't said *I love you* out loud, but she was pretty sure she'd said it nonetheless. She hoped she hadn't scared him off. "I'm sorry," she said. "I think you were expecting me to pick up at 'I feel you inside me for the first time.'"

"I like this ending better," he said, then pulled her down and kissed her. She felt a huge wave of relief. And another silent *I love you* coming on.

"Remind me again what it is I ever did to deserve a guy like you?" she asked.

Again, he did not reply. But when she pulled back, he was wearing a sleepy smile. He was contented. She was happy. "I'll go get you a blanket and pillow," she whispered, suspecting that he was already drifting off.

"Why don't you bring two pillows?" he said in a sleepy voice. "Sleep out here on the couch with me."

She kissed him lightly on the cheek. She had never fallen asleep in his arms before. Tonight was as good a night as any to start. "Okay," she said.

But when she returned a few moments later, he was already out. She gently lifted his head and inserted a pillow underneath, then crawled in next to him and pulled the blanket over their bodies.

As she snuggled into his shoulder and wrapped an arm around him, she mouthed the words silently to herself.

I love you, David.

CHAPTER 8

This sucked. She'd been in traffic before, but never like this—it was so bad that people had turned off their engines.

This is why Laura had never come to the city to see David before, even though they'd been dating for over two months now. The heat. The air quality. The traffic. But David had been making the drive to North Powell at least three times a week, and it was only fair that Laura make an effort to make the trek to see him.

Her text tone pinged. It was from Spence.

the landmark preservation office just called they want us to be there at 8 tomorrow instead of 11.

She texted back.

8? On a Saturday morning? Seriously?

seriously, he wrote.

OK (insert forlorn sigh here), see you bright and early.

see you

Phone already in hand, she called David, who picked up immediately.

"How's it going?" he said.

"I've been sitting on the interstate in my parked car for a half hour and it's about a hundred degrees. If I make it to your apartment alive, the first thing I'm doing is taking a shower. This is gross. How can you stand it?"

"My apartment has air conditioning. And an indoor pool."

"It has a pool?" she said. "As in cold water?"

"Yes."

"What's their policy on skinny-dipping? I didn't bring a bathing suit, but I'm jumping in as soon as I get there. I'll go in with my clothes on if I can't go in naked."

"There's a sportwear boutique at the end of my street. But just so you know, if you want to go swimming naked, I have no problem with that."

"Ha ha," she said, "very—oh my God, we're moving! I'll be there in fifteen."

"Okay, I'll come down to meet you in the parking lot."

Fifteen minutes later, the GPS was guiding her into the parking lot of David's building. She pulled into a spot in the back. She could see David standing at the opposite end, shielding his eyes from the sun while he scanned the lot for her car. She sent him a quick text.

I can see you.

A few moments later she received a text back. From Spence.

no you can't

Crap. She did that constantly. She typed in a quick response.

Ha ha sorry I meant to send that to David.

She was just about to hit send when she remembered who she was texting. No one at KPS was supposed to know about her and David, and this was about the tenth time she'd almost spilled the beans.

After backspacing over "David" and replacing it with "someone else," she hit send. A text from Spence saying *no problem* was just coming through when she heard a knock on her window.

"Found you," David said as he opened the car door for her.

She stepped out, and a few minutes later they were walking into the delightfully air-conditioned and very expensive-looking sportswear boutique. Laura headed to the swimwear section and went straight for the cup-sized rack. As she began examining the one-pieces, David began looking through the bikinis.

"Hey, look at this," he said, holding up a crimson double-D bikini. "All these bathing suits come with built-in breasts so you don't have to bring your own."

She grabbed the bikini out of his hand. "Shush," she said. "We're looking for a D-cup one-piece and yes, they happen to be heavily padded for extra support."

He laid a gentle hand on her shoulder, the other hand upon his heart. "Laura," he said, "I just want your breasts to know that if they ever need extra support, I'm here for them."

Despite her embarrassment, she found herself laughing. "Thank you, sir. You're such a gentleman."

But he wasn't paying attention. He was combing through the bikini rack again, intent on his mission. "How about this one?" he said. "It's a D-cup. That's what you said, right?"

It was black with purple lace overlay, and had the sort of bottom piece known in lingerie catalogs as a "cheeky" because it revealed about two inches worth of bare behind. It was more tasteful than a thong, but still unsuitable for public use as far as she was concerned. The top would fit her, but it was clearly a push-up and very skimpy. It tied at the cleavage.

"It's cute," she said. "But it looks more like something out of a fetish magazine than something I'd wear in a pool."

"I know," he said. "Isn't it great?"

"David—"

He came up closer and leaned down to whisper in her ear. "Just try it on and let me look," he said. "There's no one else in the store. All you have to do is put it on, open the door and let me look for a few minutes. And then maybe pull me inside the dressing room and lock the door and we'll just let nature take its course."

She took the hanger. "Fine," she said. "I'll try it on. But for your eyes only. There's no way I'm buying this."

It was one of those coed dressing rooms that existed only in the city, and she picked a room and closed the door behind her while David stood just outside.

After undressing and slipping on the scrap of material that made up the bikini bottoms, she slung the top around her back and adjusted the front tie and shoulder straps. Unusually complicated, it took her about five times longer than it should have to get it right.

"How is it?" David said from outside the door.

"Well," she said, "the top covers about one-eighth of my breasts and the bottoms should have the words 'bend me over a desk and do me from behind' written on them. But other than that, it's great. I'm opening the door. Is anyone else out there?"

"Just me."

"Remember, for your eyes only."

She opened the door and stood before David.

His smile disappeared.

"So?" she said.

"It's nice," he said nonchalantly. "Can I see it from the back?"

She turned around. "I'm not buying this," she said as he eyed her cheeky backside.

"Whatever," he said casually. "Hand it to me when you're done changing, I'll get it out of your way."

"Okay," she said.

She closed the door, admittedly a little disappointed at his reaction. She had a nice body and she knew it. And if nothing else, this was as close to naked as David had ever seen her. She would have liked a somewhat stronger reaction.

"Here," she said, handing him the bathing suit over the top of the door.

"Got it," he said.

She changed back into her sundress and headed back out to the cup-sized rack, expecting to find him there.

But he was not. When she looked around, she saw him at the register, paying for the bikini. She smiled. So he *did* like it on her. She was flattered, pleased, and finding herself getting a little excited right here in the store.

She met David at the register just as the clerk was handing him the bag.

"Thank you," he said as he grabbed Laura's hand and began pulling her out of the store.

"Aren't we eager?" she said.

He put his arm around her shoulder and pulled her in close. "Yes," he said with more than a little enthusiasm. "We are very eager."

They made it back to his apartment building in a matter of minutes, and a few moments later they were exiting the elevator onto the fourth floor.

"Right down here," he said.

She looked around once he'd shown her in. It was clean. Not sparkling, but clean. That much she would have expected. What she didn't expect was for it to be so well-appointed. It looked like something out of an interior design magazine.

"Wow, this is really nice," she said. "I'm impressed. I like how you have just a splash of blue against the earth tones."

When she looked up at him, it was to find him studying her.

"The bathroom's down that hall on the left, just before the office," he said. "Did you want to change into your new bathing suit now?"

"So you don't want to talk about interior decorating?"

"Perhaps some other time," he said, handing her the bag.

"I'm going to take a quick shower before I change. Give me ten minutes."

She turned down the little hallway. But before walking into the bathroom, she stole a peek at his office. It was messy, but in a good way. There were papers scattered all over his desk and a computer with dual monitors. It was the setup of a smart, hardworking man, and at the moment it was having the same effect on her as his tortoiseshell glasses had that first day they'd met. It was hot. There were two kinds of women—those who liked brawn, and those who liked brains. She was definitely the latter. And right now, his brains were making her really, really want the brawn.

She took a quick shower, changed into the bikini, and walked into the living room. But David was not there. Nor was he in the office or kitchen. That meant there was only one place he could be.

She walked into the bedroom, where the last trickle of sunlight was filtering in through the blinds. David was lying on his back on the bed, eyes closed. He was barefoot but otherwise fully dressed. He hadn't heard her come in.

"Hey, handsome," she said in a soft voice.

He opened his eyes and looked at her standing in the doorway. His focus was on her body, and his voice was quiet as he spoke. "You look really nice in that bikini."

She looked at him lying there barefoot on the blanket, his bedroom eyes intense in the dimming light.

"You look really nice on that bed."

Her response was anything but subtle. He knew that he had just heard the word "yes."

He stood up and extended an inviting hand to her. When she walked over to him, he grabbed her waist and pulled her in close. "Why don't you take that off?" he whispered in her ear, running his hands up her back.

She was not interested in undressing herself. She wanted full surrender. He was all hers, and she wanted to be all his.

"I want you to undress me," she whispered, lifting her lips for a kiss.

She felt a tingling as he ran his hands up the bare skin of her back. And as they slid down to grab her behind below her cheeky bottoms, she felt herself getting wet.

The next thing she knew, there was a slight tug at the front tie of her bikini. Then a stronger tug. And then her top opened and fell off her shoulders as David's large hands enveloped her bare breasts. He had a tender touch, and his palms caressed her in soft, lazy circles before squeezing down gently, over and over. When she felt him pinch her nipples, the tingling between her legs grew stronger and she heard herself sigh with pleasure.

In a sudden motion, he lifted her up, and in response she wrapped her legs around his waist, letting her head fall backwards as his mouth bore down on her breast. He was not shy, sucking in deeply, again and again, his teeth grazing her nipple as he laid her back on the bed. Her legs dangling over the side at the knees and her arms resting above her head, she waited for him to continue undressing her. Clothes had never been so cumbersome—she couldn't wait to be naked in his arms.

Hooking his fingers in the sides of her bikini bottoms, he pulled them down over her thighs, then over her knees, and then to the floor. He lowered himself so that he was hovering just inches above her naked body.

"You're beautiful, Laura," he said, kissing her.

His hand reached between her legs, and he began massaging her with his fingertips.

"Oh, my God," he said, dropping his head as he felt for the first time how very, very excited he made her. He moved his fingers back and forth, his wet fingertips exploring and caressing her. "Did I do this?"

She placed her hands on the back of his neck and pulled his head down to hers. "You do this to me every time you walk into the room," she said, kissing him.

Lowering himself in front of her, he embraced one of her legs. Starting at her knee, he alternated between kissing and sucking and tongue tickling, his mouth moving slowly up her thigh until she at last felt his warm breath between her legs. He moved in gently, starting with a circle of soft, teasing baby kisses. Instinctively, she reached for her breasts, caressing them with her own hands as David's mouth continued its work between her legs. She let go of one breast and grasped his head, enjoying the feel of his soft hair gliding between her fingers as his tongue traced a lazy circle around the most sensual flesh on her body. He was teasing her, making her wait for it, intentionally or not she did not know.

"David," she said, needing to hear her own voice saying his name out loud. "God, that's good."

Over and over, he pushed forward with his tongue, making her want him inside her so badly that she had to push his head away.

"Wait," she said, dropping her hips back onto the bed. She was getting too excited too fast. "If I orgasm now I won't be able to orgasm again for at least another hour and I can't wait for you that long. Just give me a minute to settle down."

He stood up and began untucking his shirt.

She pushed herself up, still a little breathless. "No," she said, grabbing his shirt. "I get to take your clothes off."

Standing on tiptoes, she pulled his shirt over his head, then pushed him onto the bed so that he was in the exact position she had been in seconds ago—on his back, his legs dangling over the side of the bed. His chest heaved with anticipation as she unbuttoned his jeans and pulled down his zipper. As she ran her fingers along the tight rim of his boxers, she laid her lips on his stomach. First just below the belly button, then a little lower, and a little lower again. There was not an inch of his body that was not utterly kiss-worthy—she wanted her mouth on every part of him.

She tugged on his jeans and pulled them down below his hips. A few more tugs, and they landed on the floor.

She looked at him, lying on his back in nothing but a pair a tight navy-blue boxers, his eyes closed, silent but for his deep breathing. Lowering herself to her knees, she tugged at his boxers, pulling them down until they joined his jeans on the pile on the floor.

His handsome face, his lean body, even his voice—everything about him was beautiful to her, always. But at this moment, naked on his back on a bed, wanting and waiting to be loved by her, he had never been so desirable. She felt like no woman on earth could want a man like she wanted David right now. And no one else could satisfy him the way she could, because no one else could want so badly to please him.

She laid her head on his stomach. She could feel his erection pressing up between her breasts as she ran one hand up his firm chest and over his shoulder before coming back down and grasping his erection. She luxuriated in the feel of his silky skin against her breasts, and she moved her body up and down so that his erection gently rubbed against one of her nipples. He let out a sigh of pleasure, and immediately her desire for him swelled—he wanted her. It made her want him more.

Holding him tenderly in her grasp, she brought the tip of his erection to her mouth, pressing it gently against her tongue, the softest caress in the world. He let out another sigh of pleasure. She knew what he wanted—to be deep in her mouth, to feel the full draw of her lips sucking him tightly, to feel her tongue rubbing up and down against his skin as he thrust in and out. But there would only be one first time. She would remember this night forever, and she wanted to preserve this moment of pure desire, this enraptured anticipation of being spectacularly satisfied. At the same time, she knew she would never be satisfied because she could never, ever get enough of this beautiful boy.

So she took her time. She pressed her lips on the tip of his erection, a warm open-mouthed kiss. She heard him inhale sharply as she traced his every contour with her tongue. She savored every second of caressing his silky skin, brushing it across her lips, and then taking the whole tip in her mouth and gently suckling. So firm yet so soft. So very lovely.

When he couldn't wait any longer, his palms gently coaxed her head downward. He arched his hips up, and she allowed her whole body to relax as he pushed himself deep into her mouth. He let out a gratified sigh as she swallowed him up, and with every thrust in, she inhaled, holding him tight, and with every pull back, she loosened the grip of her tongue. She liked it like this, his hands guiding her head as he moved in, then out, then back in again.

He did not tire easily. She drew on him harder as he began to move faster, no longer loosening the grip of her tongue as he pulled back. His audible breathing told her that he liked the feeling of resistance, her mouth pulling him back in every time he tried to pull out.

His pace began to increase, and his breathing became stilted as a delightful sound of pleasure emerged from his throat.

But then, very abruptly, he pulled out. "No," he said, seeming to be talking more to himself than to her. "Not like this."

Getting up on his knees, he reached under her arms and pulled her onto the bed until they were kneeling face to face, his arms around her waist. She loved the feel of her bare breasts against his chest, his strong hands on her bare behind, his erection pressed up against her stomach. He kissed her mouth, and then she felt his hot breath in her ear. "I want to climax inside of you," he whispered.

He kissed her hard as he lowered her onto her back, then pressed her palms down on either side of her head. As their fingers intertwined, she felt the weight of his hips upon her, and a moment later he was gliding effortlessly into her.

The moan that emerged from his throat at his first thrust told her it gave him great pleasure to feel her wet skin gripping his erection. Over and over, he thrust into her with long, deep strokes. He was the perfect size and moved at the perfect pace, and every time she felt herself clenching on him she could hear him let out a gratified sigh. It was a vicious circle of pleasure—the sound of him sighing set off another tremor inside her, her tremoring against him setting off a sigh.

She heard him let out another moan, and this time her reaction was particularly intense. As his pace increased, she felt herself on the verge of orgasm. She tried to hold off, relaxing the muscles in her legs and pelvis in hopes of keeping it at bay, but it was too late. Her legs and toes straightened, her back arched, and she contracted down on him from all sides. She had wanted to wait for him, but no matter—her own orgasm brought David to his. A deep, wonderful sound sputtered from his throat as he climaxed.

As he collapsed on top of her, she felt an over-whelming urge to tell him she loved him. But as always, the urge came with the fear that he wouldn't reciprocate.

She decided to settle for something true and real but less consequential. "David?" she said.

"Hmm?"

She caressed his back with her fingertips. "It makes me happy to make you happy."

He propped himself up on his forearms. "Then you'll be happy to know that these last couple of months with you have been the happiest of my life." He leaned down and kissed her. "Laura?" he said.

"Hmm?"

"I do believe I'm hopelessly in love with you."

Even on her back she could feel herself swoon.

"I love you, David."

When she awoke the next morning, the sun was shining brightly through the bedroom window, telling her that she had slept in later than usual. Beside her, David slept soundly.

She looked at the bedside clock. 8:15 a.m. She estimated that they had fallen asleep at about ten last night, which meant he'd been asleep for over ten hours. She thought of what he'd been saying about the stress at work lately, and how he'd been plagued by insomnia for two weeks straight. But last night, wrapped in her arms with his head upon their shared pillow, he had finally gotten a full night's rest. Earth-shattering lovemaking, followed by a romantic dinner at home, followed by more cataclysmic sex, topped off with a long and well-deserved rest. He was anything but a chore, but she felt like she had done her job well.

She felt him starting to shift. After a labored stretch, he opened his eyes.

"Hey, sleeping beauty," she said. "Did you sleep well?"

"I slept great," he said. "Better than I have in weeks. You?"

"Like a baby.

On the nightstand next to David, her phone rang.

"Ignore it," she said.

But it was too late. David glanced at the caller ID. "Markham," he grumbled. "Do you see what I mean about this guy? He somehow figured out that I'm relaxing in bed next to a beautiful woman for the first time in two years and decided he needed to be a part of it. I'm telling you, this guy is the biggest pain in the ass—"

"My phone please?"

"—in the long and storied history of my ass. An elbow pipe up my ass would be less painful. A fireplace poker—"

"Can I please have my phone? It might be important."

"What could possibly be so important that he's calling at eight o'clock on a Saturday morning?"

Grabbing the phone out of David's hand, she leapt out of bed.

"Oh my God, Spence, I was supposed to meet you at eight. I completely forgot. Oh my God, I'm so sorry. Oh my God, oh my God."

"It's okay," he said. "As soon as I got here they told me they'd bumped the meeting back to nine thirty, but we definitely need your paperwork for the meeting. How soon can you get here?"

"An hour?"

"Okay, that should give us enough time."

"Thank you, Spence. And sorry again. I'll be there soon."

When she sat back down on the bed, David was looking at her with raised eyebrows.

"Remember that text Spence sent me about landmarking Powell House a few weeks ago?" she said.

"How could I forget? Mr. Impeccable Timing himself."

"His dad got us an appointment with the Landmark Preservation Committee. I was supposed to meet him at eight but I completely forgot. I'm really sorry."

David sighed deeply. "It's okay, sweetheart. I know how important this is to you." His tone of voice was patient, but it was clear that he was less than thrilled that their perfect night had culminated with a wake-up call from one of his least favorite people on earth. "I guess it's nice to know Markham's good for something."

"I'll let him know you said that," she said. "It'll be the biggest compliment he's gotten from you since 'He's not as stupid as he looks.' I'm going to grab a quick shower."

"Before you hop in," David said, "just one little thing."

"Yeah?" she said, a little nervous.

"Just so you know, I'm not mad or anything. But going forward, can I ask that you please not talk to my male coworkers," he said, gesturing to her body, "when you're naked?"

Oh, right. That.

"If it makes you feel better, this is only the third or fourth time I've talked to one of your coworkers while I'm naked. Fifth, tops."

He pulled her down on top of him. "You know," he said, "if you're already going to be an hour late, you may as well be an hour and ten minutes late."

Through the sheet that was separating his naked body from hers, she could feel his erection pressing up against her pelvis. "Didn't you get enough last night?"

"I'm just requesting ten minutes of your time," he said, kissing her neck. "You won't even notice I'm here."

Laura laughed. "I can't keep Spence waiting any longer than I already have."

But as soon as David pulled the sheet out from between them and she felt his warm naked body under hers, Spence became a lost cause. Before she knew it, she was straddling David's hips and he was sinking into her for the third time in sixteen hours.

It was simply amazing what one man could accomplish in the course of a single day.

CHAPTER 9

She pulled into the parking lot and looked at the dashboard clock. 9:10. The meeting with the Landmark Preservation Committee started in twenty minutes, which meant Spence would be expecting her in five. She had just enough time to make a very quick call to David.

"Hey, you," he said, picking up. "Isn't there a landmark committee you're supposed to be fawning over? Perhaps offering a minor kickback to?"

"Shoot, they're going to be expecting a kickback? I was just going to offer sex."

"Ha ha. Tell anyone that if they come within ten feet of my woman, I'll come there and break some legs."

"Will do. Anyhow, I only have thirty seconds, but I just really wanted to tell you I love you again before the meeting."

"I love you again before the meeting, too, beautiful. Also, I'll probably be willing to love you again after the meeting. When will you be home?"

"A few hours?" she said.

"See you then," he said. "Good luck."

"Thank you!"

She stuck her phone in her briefcase and exited her car. Despite Spence's repeated assurances that there was nothing to worry about, she still felt nervous. All they were doing today was giving a ten-minute presentation to the committee and then handing off the "pre-application," which was an application to determine whether or not they were eligible to submit an application.

She started walking across the parking lot. The building they were meeting at reminded her of North Powell's town hall, but bigger. And like town hall, it was old and a little beat-up, with potholes all over the parking lot. Unlike town hall, however, it had a playground on one side and a basketball court on the other.

The latter was where she spotted Spence. He was wearing a pressed baby-blue business shirt, a pair of neat gray slacks, and black business shoes. It was the most well-dressed she'd ever seen him, which was ironic given he was currently wearing this very fine outfit while shooting baskets. She put her briefcase on the bench, and then headed to the court.

"Hey, Laura," he said when he finally saw her.

"Hello, Mr. Markham," she said. "Don't you clean up nice." She gestured to the basketball in his hand. "You're good. Did you play in college?"

"High school," he said. "You?"

"Seriously?" she said. "Most of the time I can't even throw the ball high enough to reach the basket."

He tossed the basketball at her. She reacted the same way she did back in gym class: by shielding herself from the impending blow.

"Sorry," Spence said as the basketball bounced off her forearms. After scooping it up and tucking it under one arm, he came over and positioned her hands in front of her, palms up. He then very gingerly handed her the ball.

"See how easy that was?" Laura said. "I never understood why the other girls in class had to surround me like a bunch of hyenas and wrestle the ball away when all they had to do was ask politely and I would have gladly given it to them. 'Excuse me, Laura, may I please borrow the ball?' 'Why, certainly, Claire. May I have it back when you're finished?' 'Of course, Laura, it would rude of me not to share.'"

Spence wisely chose not to argue with her bold new take on basketball etiquette. "Would you like to take a turn throwing the ball into the basket, Miss Delaney?"

"How nice of you to offer, Mr. Markham."

She wandered around in her high heels, trying to find the best position from which to attempt a shot. After settling into a spot about six feet from the basket, she placed one hand on the side of the ball and the other hand on the bottom, the way she'd seen real basketball players do it. She tossed it forward.

Spence jogged ahead to retrieve the basketball from the grass beyond the court.

"Let's try to be a little less ambitious this time," he said as he handed the ball back to her. "Don't worry about making a basket. If you can get the ball to hit the backboard, we'll consider it a victory."

She again strategically positioned herself in front of the basket. Once again, she attempted her shot.

Spence trotted over to the lawn and grabbed the ball again.

"Okay," he said. "Let's try something different. Do you remember how to dribble?"

"I'm not a complete idiot, Spence. I know how to bounce a ball."

"I'm going to stand behind you. Dribble the ball a couple of times and then shoot."

"Fine," she said.

Walking slowly toward the basket, she bounced the ball—or *dribbled*, as men insisted on saying. When she came to within about three feet of the basket, she raised her hands to shoot. But just as she was about to let go of the ball, she felt two hands on her hips and her body being lifted about four feet straight up in the air.

Instinctively, she dropped the ball and twisted around to wrap her arms tightly around Spence's head, holding on for dear life.

She could hear him laughing.

"I'm sorry," Spence said once she'd slid down his body and back to the ground. "I should have warned you." He picked up the ball once again and handed it to her. "Okay, here's what we'll do. You walk toward the basket and dribble the ball three times. After the third bounce, I'm going to lift you up and you shoot. Good?"

"Good," Laura said. "Let's give it a try."

She bounced the ball three times. This time she was ready when Spence's hands grabbed her hips and lifted her up. "Should I shoot now?" she asked, her toes four feet above the ground.

"Yes," he said.

"Can you get me a little closer?"

He took two steps forward.

"Actually can we stand right in front of the basket? I think that—"

"My arms are getting tired."

She threw the ball. And cried out with absolute glee when it went through the basket.

"I did it!" she cried as Spence lowered her to the ground. "Did you see that? I think that's the first time in my life I actually got the ball in the basket!"

"Great job," he said, high-fiving her. "You're the next LeBron James."

"Who?"

"Never mind," he said. "Should we get ready for the meeting?"

"I guess we should," she said.

They walked over to the bench and sat down.

"So," Spence said, "my dad suggested sticking to the facts and keeping it short. We can wait to argue the merits until after they've approved the pre-application."

"I'll take your dad's word for it," she said, pulling an envelope out of her briefcase. "So I've got everything you said we needed. The inspection certificate, proof of properly installed plumbing and HVAC, and a list from the contractor of all the stuff that still needs to be done. I also got these from the town hall archives," she said, pulling some very old photos out of the envelope. "This is the house over a hundred years ago."

Spence took the stack from her hand. "Wow," he said. "So this is it before the wraparound porch was added. It's weird to see it so . . . what's the word?"

"Inhabitable?"

"That's the word. And no street or anything. It's just standing out in the middle of a field all by itself."

"I know," she said. "And look at that tree in the front yard."

"This little one here?" he said.

"Yeah. I'm pretty sure that's the massive tree in the front yard that's responsible for all the squirrels in the attic."

Just then, the reminder tone pinged on Spence's phone. "Ten minutes," he said. "Better get ready." He handed the pictures back to Laura before grabbing his tie out of his briefcase. "Just let me tie this," he said, attempting to thread the wide end through the loop. "I'll be done in five minutes. Ten, tops. Hope you brought a book."

After a full minute of watching him fumble, she extended a hand, trying not to laugh. "May I?" she said.

He pulled the tie off his neck and handed it over. "Be my guest," he said.

She held it out horizontally in front of him. "Narrow end to the left, wide end to the right," she said. She looped the tie around his neck and used the two ends to pull him in closer to her. "Step one," she said, buttoning the top button of his shirt, "you actually have to button this."

"It's uncomfortable."

"You can unbutton it as soon as you talk these people into signing off on our pre-application. I'll even unbutton it for you. It'll be your reward."

"Thank you."

"Step two," she said, pushing his collar up. "Wide end should be longer than the narrow."

"It's uncomfortable," he said again.

"I didn't even tie it yet. Hold still and pay attention." She brought the two ends to his throat and continued her demonstration. "And last but not least," she said, "we push up the knot to your throat."

"Shouldn't I be able to breathe?" he said, squirming.

"I say again—you can breathe as soon as you talk these people into signing off on our pre-application." She folded down his collar, then smoothed out his shirt at his shoulders for no particular reason except that she'd seen women do it in TV shows from the 1950s.

"Want to give it a try?" she said.

"I'll have a go at it, but don't get your hopes up."

She untied his tie, pulled it from his neck and handed it back. "Okay, let's see it."

He put the tie around his neck and began his first attempt at tying it. "How am I doing so far?"

"The tie goes under your collar, not over it," she said, pushing his collar up for him. "I'm not sure how you lived thirty-one years without noticing that part. But otherwise, you're doing great."

"Good, because I already forgot the rest."

"Wide end longer," she said.

When he had pulled the two ends of his tie to the appropriate lengths, she verbally guided him through the steps again. "Almost there," she said as he pulled the completed Windsor knot up as far as it would go, which was about mid-chest.

"Perfect," he said. "Should we head inside?"

She grabbed the end of his tie and loosened the knot. After pulling and tugging a little, she was able to slide the knot up to his throat. "Now it's perfect," she said.

"Thank you," he said.

"My pleasure. Ready for the meeting?"

"Not really," he said. "But at least I look ready. That's a step in the right direction. Shall we?"

"Let's do it."

Just as they were grabbing their briefcases, Spence's text tone pinged. He held out his phone for Laura to read.

Sorry Mr. Spencer running late mtg changed to 11.

She looked at him. "At least they got your name rightish."

"I've never been fussy," he said, already untying his tie. "Spence Markham, Mark Spenceham. Ham Spencemark. I learned a long time ago to settle for close enough."

"Alright, what do we do for the next hour and a half?"

"We could play some more basketball."

"Seriously, what do we do for the next hour and a half?"

"I think I saw a diner a few doors down. Am I allowed to eat or do I have to wait until I've talked these people into signing off on our pre-application?"

She pretended to think it over. "Fine," she said. "You can eat. But don't get used to it."

A few minutes later they were taking their seats at the crowded diner.

"Here's a question," Spence said after they ordered their coffees. "How did you learn to tie a tie?"

"From my mom. Old-fashioned girl. Before I left for college she insisted on teaching me how to tie a man's tie."

"Really?" Spence said. "That surprises me. Didn't you tell me your mom owns her own successful business? She doesn't sound like the type to send her daughter off to college to get her MRS degree."

"She is and she isn't. She and my dad got married right after they graduated college and I was born a year later. Their plan was to have four kids and he would work and she would be a stay-at-home mom. But then he died when they were twenty-seven and that was pretty much the end of that plan. She took a job at an insurance agency, learned the ropes, and a few years later opened her own company."

"Oh my God," Spence said. "That's awful." He was wearing that horrified look everyone wore when she was forced to tell the dreaded "widow and orphan" story. "I mean the part where your father died," he said, clarifying, "not the insurance part."

"I knew what you meant," she said. "And I'm sure it was awful. But I was four. I doubt I even understood."

"Do you have any memories of him?"

"Just one," she said. "Do you know this song 'The Band Played On'? It's from like 1910 or something."

"Yeah, I know that song. *He'd ne'er leave the girl with the strawberry curls, and the band played on.*"

She said nothing, just looked at him from across the table. "Oh my God."

"Please don't say it," he said.

"Did anyone ever tell you that you have a really nice singing voice?"

"I just asked you not to say it."

"And it did you absolutely no good, did it? I just went ahead and said it anyway."

He gave her a fake and very unconvincing dirty look.

"And yes, you got the song right," she said. "We had this nightly ritual before bed. He'd sit me on his hip and waltz me around the room while he sang it to me. I thought the whole song was about me."

"You thought you were the girl with the strawberry curls?" Spence said.

"Yes. And please don't say it."

Spence leaned back in his chair, laughing. "That's really cute."

"I just asked you not to say it."

"And it did you absolutely no good, did it? I just went ahead and took my revenge anyway."

Laura gave him a fake dirty look.

"But seriously," Spence said, "I have three nieces, so I know cute. It's not quite as cute as Bonnie and Becca calling me 'Uncle Pants', though."

"Uncle Pants?" Laura repeated, laughing. "But I—wait," she said as she realized something. "Aren't James's two oldest daughters named Bonnie and Becca?"

"Yeah," Spence said, looking a little confused at her confusion.

"So James's daughters have the same name as your nieces?"

"James's daughters are my nieces," he said. "James is my brother-in-law. I thought you knew that."

"I had no idea," Laura said. But then she remembered back to their second meeting. Spence had been talking to James's daughter on the phone and James was complaining that his kids listened to Spence but not to him. "But now that I think of it," she said, "that meeting we had in the sewing room, I did think it was kind of odd that you said 'I love you' to your coworker's kid."

"Yeah," he said. "Believe it or not we're very tight. He's the reason I'm at KPS. We were roommates in college. He had an analyst job lined up at KPS and I had a job lined up at an engineering firm. But my firm went out of business a month before I graduated. James still owed me for not murdering him when he got my eighteen-year-old sister pregnant, so he got me an interview with Creative Services. The rest is history."

Laura just sat there, floored. "James got your eighteen-year-old sister pregnant? Do I want to know the details?"

"The short version is that Bethany came to visit me one weekend toward the end of my senior year in college. She arrived on Friday night and by Sunday morning she was pregnant."

"What's the long version?"

"The long version is that I decided to let James live."

Laura laughed, and didn't dig further. The mental image of the nerdy James Murphy getting a barely legal teenager pregnant was not a pretty one.

The waitress was just bringing them their coffees when Spence's text tone pinged again. "You've got to be kidding me," he said as he showed the text to Laura.

Hi Mark we had a change in schedule can you be here at 9:45?

"We should be able to make it if we leave right now," Laura said.

Spence threw a ten dollar bill on the table and they rushed out before their coffees were even served. Five minutes later they were back in the parking lot.

"Tie," Laura said. "Remember what I taught you?"

"No," he said. "Can you just do it?"

She placed her briefcase on the hood of a random car. Once again, she buttoned his top button and tied a proper Windsor knot for him. "Perfect," she said. "Let's try this again."

They walked through the front door of the old building and stopped at the reception desk.

"Can I help you?" said the woman behind the counter.

"Yes, Laura Delaney and Mark Spencer here to see Doug Waterson," Spence said casually.

Laura dropped her head to hide her smile.

The receptionist looked at her computer. "Just a moment," she said, picking up the receiver of an old-fashioned desktop phone and punching in three digits. "Bridget? Doug's 9:45 is here." She hung up her phone. "Bridget will be right with you," she said. "You can wait over there on the bench."

They took their seats. A few minutes later a fortysomething woman with very loud shoes came walking toward them.

"Mr. Spencer," she said, extending her hand for a shake before turning to Laura. "Mrs. Spencer. How nice to meet you both. We're really sorry for all the schedule changes, it's been a crazy morning. Do you have the paperwork we discussed?"

Laura opened her briefcase and took out her stack of papers. "I've got the inspection reports and also some photos that show a little bit of the history of the house. I'll get you the architectural plans as soon as I track them down." She turned to Spence. "Honey, do you have the application?"

"Yes, dear," he replied, opening his briefcase and handing the paperwork to Bridget.

Bridget gathered up all their paperwork into a neat pile. "Great," she said. "I'm going to bring these to the committee. We'll look them over at our monthly meeting, and if we think your home is a candidate for landmark status, we'll be in touch. Thank you again for coming."

With that, she turned and walked away.

The Spencers just stood there, struck dumb.

Finally, Laura turned to her husband. "Is that it?" she said.

"Thank you for coming," the receptionist interrupted, nodding toward the exit. "We'll be in touch."

"Yeah," Mark said to his wife. "I'm pretty sure that's it."

When they reached her car, Laura turned to Spence. "I'm really sorry you drove all this way and wore nice shoes and a button-down shirt for nothing."

"It won't be for nothing," he said. "It'll just take a while. We knew that from the beginning."

"Still," she said, "if I'd known that all we were going to do was hand over papers, I would have done it myself. You gave up your Saturday." She tugged at his least-favorite article of clothing. "You wore a tie." She knew none of this was her fault, but she felt terribly, terribly guilty. "Can I make it up to you with dinner on Monday night? I can make you that Cajun chicken and rice dish that you liked."

"Only if you insist."

"I insist."

"Fine," he said. "See you Monday. Meet at Powell House?"

"As always," she said. "And don't forget the rotary sander."

"It's already in my Jeep," he said. "Drive safe."

"You too."

She got back into her car and began driving back to David's place. She hadn't had sex in over two hours.

She hoped he was ready for round four.

CHAPTER 10

It had been just about two months since they submitted the landmark pre-application to the state, and they still hadn't heard a peep back. At this point she cared less about the landmark status itself than the restoration grants that she hoped would open up along with it. Laura was proud of the labor costs she and Spence were saving by doing work with their own hands, but materials cost money. They needed cash.

She opened the front door to Powell House and walked inside.

"Spence?" she called. "Are you here?" She stuck her head into the library, or as she and Spence had jokingly nicknamed it, "headquarters." But he was not there. "Spence?"

She looked at the time. Four thirty. David had stuck a weekly Monday morning meeting on Spence's calendar, so he'd been coming to North Powell in the afternoons these last few weeks. Still, he was usually here by four. Maybe he'd hit traffic.

She decided to get down to business on her own—if what she and Spence did here on Mondays deserved to be called "business" at all. The town's new webpage was scheduled to go live on November 1st, just a few weeks from today, and the planning for the Dickens Festival was in full swing. But the truth was, most of her and Spence's work on Dickens was done outside business hours. They spent the bulk of their Mondays together at Powell House, sanding floors and laying tiles and installing new sinks, then followed it with dinner at Laura's. Helping her restore a broken-down house was nowhere in Spence's contract, and making sure he got a decent homecooked meal once a week was the least she could do in return.

She went into the closet, got her gardening basket, and walked out the back door, where she practically tripped over Spence. He was sitting on the back step with his laptop on his knees, dressed in his finest work attire—jeans, his beat-up sneakers, and a gray jersey with an unbuttoned flannel over top.

"God, Spence, you have to stop scaring me like this. Start making more noise," she said as she took a seat beside him.

He was composing an email to a client. "Speaking of next year," he said, looking at his laptop screen, "I'm wondering if we should think about advertising for Valentine's Day during Dickens."

She looked around for whoever it was he was talking to. But they were alone. "Were we speaking of next year?"

"No," he said, still typing. "But I was talking to myself before you got here."

She had a flashback to the first time they met in the sewing room. "You're so freaking weird, man," she said, repeating James's sentiment of so many months ago.

He nudged her teasingly with his elbow. "How is me talking to myself any weirder than you talking to a house?"

She elbowed him back. Hard.

"What?" he said.

"Nothing," she said. "I just felt like assaulting you in a menacing yet playful way."

He hit send, closed his laptop, and finally focused on her. "What do you think about the B and Bs maybe handing out fliers for Valentine's Day while people are here for Dickens? Book a room before December 6th and get twenty percent off. Stuff like that."

She had never thought of North Powell as a Valentine's Day hot spot. But they did have plenty of romantic restaurants and almost every B and B room had a queen bed.

"That's okay," he said when she did not respond to his question. "You don't have to answer me verbally. Just punch me in the nose for yes and kick me in the shin for no."

She caressed the bridge of his nose in three gentle strokes.

"So you like it," he said.

"I love it," she said. "Best nose ever."

She could see him trying not to laugh. "Yeah, okay," he said. "I'm the weird one."

Despite her silly mood, she couldn't deny that Spence's idea was one worth pondering. "Do you really think people might want to come to North Powell as a romantic destination?"

Usually Spence had a lot of confidence in his own ideas. But she knew him well enough by now to recognize the look on his face: he was doubting himself.

"I don't know, actually," he said, rethinking the matter. "We're promoting the town as a family destination and Valentine's is couples only. I think that might be the one time you might be in direct competition with Haven. James and David and I did the marketing for the Haven Hot Springs grand opening, and I can tell you that Valentine's is the most popular time of year for hot-tubbing and couples massages and all that."

"God, it's just so frustrating," Laura said. "Don't get me wrong, I love that we're promoting North Powell as a wholesome family destination, but I just feel like no matter what we do, we're always going to be Haven and Bainbridge's ugly stepsister. We just can't compete."

"Well," Spence said, "to a certain extent you're right. Realistically there's nothing here that can compete with natural hot springs."

"Well, there's the North Powell hot springs," she said. "If we decided to exploit them, we could compete. But unlike Haven and Bainbridge, North Powell chooses to retain its soul rather than fatten its wallet."

She looked over at Spence to find him staring at her blankly. Suddenly, she remembered who she was talking to. She and Spence had become so chummy over the last few months that she sometimes forgot that his official role in her life was that of marketing guru, not confidante. His job was to make money for his clients. And she had just spilled the beans that North Powell was sitting on a potential gold mine.

"I didn't imagine it, right?" he finally said. "You did just say that North Powell has natural hot springs?"

"Don't even think of it, Spence," she said. "It's not an option. I'm speaking on behalf of the whole town when I say that. Haven used to be a nice little community. Family-owned shops and restaurants. Homes, churches, families who'd lived there generation after generation. Now those people can't even afford to live in the trailer parks for the seasonal employees. The town pool is now a members-only spa and the synagogue is a disco."

He stood up and folded his arms across his chest. After all these months of observing KPS's best idea guy in action, she knew his moods and mannerisms well. This was his problem-solving pose. He was about to start tapping his right elbow.

"Listen, Laura," he said, tapping his right elbow. "Don't get me wrong, the Dickens Festival is going to be great and the local businesses are going to make a killing. For *three days*. Hot springs are a three-hundred-and-sixty-five-day cash cow. And I'm not just talking about the money the springs themselves would bring in. The B and Bs could double their rates and still be filled to capacity year round. Main Street would have more shoppers than it could handle—"

"And North Powell as we know it would disappear forever," she said. "We've thought about it, Spence, believe me. Commercializing the hot springs has been a topic of debate at town meetings since about 1930. And since 1930, we've been unanimously voting it down."

He sat back down at her side. "I understand what you're saying," he said. "I do. And I'm not going to try to make you or anyone in this town do anything they don't want to do. But can I just say one more thing?"

She nodded, looking down. "Sure."

"The difference between the Dickens Festival and the hot springs? It's like the difference between a Band-Aid and a heart transplant. You hired KPS to keep North Powell from bleeding to death and that's what Dickens is going to do. But commercializing the hot springs will give this town a whole new lease on life. You won't just be able to fix the high school roof. You'll be able to build a whole new school. With art and music teachers. You could fund a new library." He thumbed toward the back door of Powell House. "You could start a town museum. And that would be just the beginning."

He was right. She knew that. But knowing the truth and accepting it were two different things. Denial was the most underrated stage of the grieving process. She of all people should know. She'd been happily stagnating in it for about five years now.

She stood up and pulled some gardening scissors out of her bag. "I'm going to clear out those weeds over by the fence," she said, avoiding eye contact.

He grabbed a spade out of the bag. "Let me help. We need to get them out by the roots or they'll grow back in a week."

They spent the next forty-five minutes silently pulling weeds while Laura tried to pretend that the hot springs conversation had never happened. Spence very thoughtfully went along with the act.

But as their silence approached the one-hour mark, Laura couldn't take it anymore. She'd known from the beginning that if she told KPS about the hot springs, they'd be all over it like white on rice. Her silence on the matter had been calculated and deliberate. But now she felt like she'd lied to Spence. He'd more than proven himself worthy of her trust. And in return, she'd deliberately kept secrets from him. She stabbed her gardening scissors into the dirt, pulled her phone out of her skirt pocket, and looked at the time. 4:45.

"Are you in any kind of hurry to get back to the city?" she asked.

"Me?" he said. "I'm never in a hurry to get back to the city."

She stood up. "You deserve a sunset," she said. "What do you think about skipping dinner tonight and going for a hike? We'd have to walk back in the dark, so if you're not experienced—"

"Best idea I've heard in a year," he said, standing up. "Let's do it."

He grabbed a few bottles of water from the kitchen as Laura converted her purse into a backpack. She pulled a flashlight out of one of the drawers and added it to the bag.

"I'll carry that," Spence said.

Five minutes later, they were at the trailhead. The last time she'd been hiking was back in June, when David had made it less than one quarter of the way up Octopus Trail. She smiled as she looked at the trail before her now. Called Death Trap, it was rocky, steep, and overgrown. Most tourists didn't even know the path existed, and city folk generally turned tail and ran back the way they came as soon as they saw the "Caution: Rattlesnake Nesting" sign.

She and Spence began down the path. The trail's initial incline was moderate, but it was rocky and narrow and they had to push a lot of branches out of the way.

"You still good?" she asked Spence when they were about a quarter mile in.

"I'm good," he said.

"You go in front of me," she said, making space for him to pass. "There are a few spots where I'll need you to help me."

After about a hundred yards of ascending, the path suddenly ended in a steep incline. Grabbing a branch for support, Spence turned to Laura. "Did I go off-path?"

"No," she said.

Still holding onto the branch, he looked at the thick trees, rocks, and brambles in confusion. The sunlight was just barely making its way through the dense treetops. "Is this where we watch the sunset?"

"No," she said. "This is how we keep the best sunset-viewing spot in a hundred square miles a secret from the public."

He raised an eyebrow. "No path?"

"No path," she said, holding out her hand. "This is one of those spots where I need some help."

Once he'd found solid footing, they grabbed each other's wrists and he pulled her up.

"Don't worry," she assured him once she was next to him again. "I've done this a million times. Just be careful not to let me die before nightfall. You'll never find your way back alone."

He followed behind her as they hiked—and some-times climbed—another half-mile through the woods. At last they reached a clearing at the top of the mountain, at which point Laura sat down on the grass. After dropping the backpack, Spence sat down next to her.

"This is really nice," he said, catching his breath. "A lot of work to get here, but it was worth it."

"This is just a way station," she said. "We still have about a half-mile to go. You up to it?"

"I'm up to it," Spence answered. "Where exactly are we headed?"

"Down," she said, pointing to the valley below.

Spence looked down the side of the mountain. "No path, I suppose?"

"Of course not."

Once again, Spence followed behind as Laura led the way. The climb down was much easier than the climb up, and twenty minutes later they emerged from the deep woods into a vast clearing. Now that they were out of the trees, they could hear the soothing trickle of the slow-moving river below. Directly across from them was an enormous and almost perpendicular slab of solid rock.

"Granite Mountain?" Spence asked.

"The one and only. This time of year the sun sets right between those two mountains over there on the right. But we're not quite to our final destination yet," she said. "Follow me."

They made their way downhill, following the natural path that had formed between a series of large and foreboding rocks.

At last, they were there.

Spence looked around in awe. "Oh my God," he said. "This is unbelievable."

"Welcome to the unnamed and unadvertised hot springs of North Powell," she said.

Spence dropped the backpack to the ground, then stretched out on his stomach on the large flat rock that extended over the water. He stuck his head out over the edge and Laura lay on her stomach beside him. They gazed down upon the clear, steaming waters of the hot spring ten feet below.

"How warm is it?" he asked her.

"A hundred degrees," she said. "I assume you want to get closer?"

"Yes," he said, standing back up.

"This way," Laura said, climbing back to her feet and then leading the way to a series of flat rocks that made a makeshift staircase down to the springs. "You go first."

When they were close to the bottom, she called for him to stop. The last "step" was about a five-foot drop.

"It rained this morning so the rocks will probably still be slippery," she explained. "When the rocks are wet, you hold that root to your left, sit on the edge, and then jump. Then I'll need you to help me get down."

Spence did as told, and then turned around. Laura was sitting on the step with her legs dangling over the edge.

He reached up and grabbed her firmly at the hips. "You're right, the rocks are slippery, so let's take it slow," he said. "Ready?"

"Ready," she said. She slid, rather than jumped, and held on to his shoulders as he lowered her down with ease. Then she led him to the dry rocks of the outer pool.

"This is a good spot," she said, sitting down on a large slab. As she lay down on her back, her wraparound skirt slid open over her leg. She could feel the warmth of the evening sun against her bare thigh as she wiggled her toes in the warm waters of the pool below. There was nothing as satisfying as spring waters after a strenuous hike, and she was sorely tempted to strip down to her underwear and jump in.

As she pulled out her scrunchie and let her hair spill out over her shoulders, Spence lay down beside her. Her bare thigh pressed lightly against his leg.

"It's still about an hour until sunset," she said quietly so as not to disrupt the tranquility of the moment. "You okay with doing nothing for that long? I know how much you hate to hold still."

"I'm great with doing nothing for that long," he said, his voice equally hushed. "It's only when I'm at work that I get fidgety. I can't even remember the last time I felt this peaceful." He was quiet for a few moments. "I can't even remember the last time I used the word peaceful. Certainly not since I started working at KPS."

She looked over at him. He was lying on his back with one hand under his head and the other resting on his stomach. His eyes were closed, and he was smiling just a little.

"Spence?" she said.

"Hmm?"

"Don't you like your job?"

"At the moment?" he said. "At the moment it's the best job in the world. But tomorrow I have to spend the entire day at an exotic car dealership pretending that I think a quarter of a million dollars is a reasonable price to pay for a car that has no back seat. But even then, I don't hate it. I just wish I had more clients who said things like *you deserve a sunset.*"

She continued to study him. He looked like he sounded. Peaceful.

"You're smiling," she said.

His eyes remained closed. "I must be happy."

She felt a swell of emotion. It was the same flicker of joy she felt anytime she heard the words "I'm happy" spoken by someone in her personal care. Mom. David. And now, evidently, Spence.

"I'm glad you like it here," she said. "I was worried that you were going to be bored to death working with such a trivial client."

"Are you kidding?" he said, turning his head. "I've been at KPS since I was twenty-one and this is the first time I've ever felt like I'm doing something worthwhile. Like whether I succeed or fail has a consequence beyond whether a bunch of investors are going to see their shares rise ten percent or fifteen percent in the coming year."

A few clouds were rolling in, which was good news for the sunset. But her moment of joy was over, suffocated by a sense of foreboding. And more than a little self-blame.

"Do you think I'm in denial?" she said.

He opened his eyes, seeming surprised. "How do you mean?"

"I know the kind of money the hot springs could bring to this town. I've always known. And I know perfectly well that the Dickens Festival alone isn't going to be near enough to get us back on our feet. But I think when I heard you use the words 'bleeding to death' it was kind of an eye-opener."

"Crap," he said, sitting up. "This is why I try to keep my mouth shut and let James and David do the talking. Don't listen to anything I say."

"You were right."

"Maybe. But that doesn't mean you're wrong in wanting to preserve the town. And just to be clear, the plan behind the Dickens Festival isn't just to make money for three days and then be over and done with. What we want is for the people who come to Dickens to fall in love with North Powell so that they'll keep coming back. That's why I was talking about advertising for Valentine's while they're here for Dickens. And during Valentine's, we promote the butterfly pavilion, and while people are here for the butterfly pavilion, we hype summer recreation. And so on."

"And you think that will be enough?"

He grimaced, clearly ambivalent.

"You have the world's worst poker face."

He nodded. "So I'm told."

He lay down and rolled onto his side, propping his head in his hand. "We don't have to have all the answers right now. If Dickens works the way we hope and it increases tourism throughout the year, then we might just be able to keep the springs a secret."

She rolled over so that she was facing him. "When was the last time I said thank you?"

"For what?" he said. "I'm just doing my job."

"No," she said. "You're not. I'm paying KPS about a thousand times less than what your other clients pay and yet I take up about twenty percent of your work week. That can't be a good use of your time and talent. Why do you do it?"

He smiled that contented little smile again. "Like I said," he said. "I must be happy."

She rolled onto her back. There was something she wanted to say to him, but it was kind of embarrassing. She closed her eyes so she could say it without looking at him.

"Can I confess something?" she said.

"Yes?" he said cautiously.

"When James first said you'd be coming here on Mondays, I was resentful. I didn't want to give up my day off. But now Mondays are my official favorite day of the week and I don't know what I'm going to do when . . ."

She trailed off. When he said nothing, she took a moment, trying to find the right words.

"What I mean is that you keep talking about how 'we'll' promote North Powell year-round. 'We'll' promote Valentine's and hype summer fun. But the truth is that your job here will be finished once Dickens ends. And that will be it. It'll be over." The weight of her own words suddenly hit her. "You'll be gone, Spence. What am I supposed to do without you?"

Spence remained silent beside her. She wished he would say something. The quiet was deafening.

She opened her eyes, expecting to find him still on his side with his head propped up on his hand. Instead she found him on his back, his eyes closed, his clenched fists pressed against his forehead.

"Spence?" she said, sitting up. "I'm sorry, did I say something wrong?"

"You didn't say anything wrong," he said, the tension in his body invading his voice as he attempted to fake a smile. "I'm just thinking about work. A different client. Not you."

She suddenly felt an overwhelming need to comfort him. This was the first time she had seen him look remotely unhappy, and she didn't like it. Reaching down, she brushed his hair away from his forehead.

"The hot springs are a designated stress-free zone," she said as she let her fingers glide through his hair. "If you're going to be unhappy, I'm going to have to ask you to leave. And as I mentioned before, you'll never find your way back alone. So those are your options. Stop thinking stressful thoughts or die alone in the woods."

He kept his eyes closed, but he smiled, this time a little more believably. "I choose to live."

"Good choice," she whispered. A little reluctantly, she untangled her fingers from his hair and lay back down beside him. She felt the smooth granite beneath her back, the soothing waters of the springs tickling her toes, and the warmth of Spence's body just barely brushing against hers. In the not too far distance, she could hear the river trickling downstream.

"If I nod off," she said, "can you wake me up before the sunset?"

"I will if I'm awake."

As always, the springs were inspiring a state of extreme relaxation, and she found herself drifting off to sleep at Spence's side.

The next thing she felt was a hand on her thigh, giving a gentle squeeze. Waking with a jolt, she looked up to find Spence beside her. "How long was I out?" she asked.

"I'm not sure," he said. "I dozed off, too."

She sat herself upright and rubbed her eyes. "I think I had a dream about you," she said.

"Really?" he said. "What was it about?"

"I don't remember exactly," she said. "But there was a turkey involved."

"Thank you," he said. "That's exactly what every man wants to hear when a woman tells him she was dreaming of him."

Laura laughed, realizing how stupid she'd sounded. "If it helps, it was a really nice turkey. He lent you a deck of cards and you lost all of the sevens, but he wasn't mad at you at all."

"Yes, that helps," Spence said. "I feel much better knowing that I spent your dream in the company of a merciful turkey."

"I'll try to program my subconscious to dream of you winning the lottery next time," she said.

"Thank you."

She looked to her left, where the sun was beginning its descent. "If we hop one step down, we can sit a little more comfortably."

"Let me go first," Spence said, jumping down. Without her needing to ask, he reached up for her hand to help her down.

"Right here," she said, crawling under the overhang and sitting with her back against the granite. "It's like theatre seating. Backrest and everything."

They sat silently as the sun made its descent in the western sky. It was about as perfect as a sunset could be—all the right hues, and just enough clouds to reflect the last lingering rays of the sun, but not so many that they obscured the view of the mountains. Out of the corner of her eye, she kept watch on Granite Mountain, waiting for the perfect moment.

When the sun was hovering just above the horizon, she nudged Spence with her elbow. "Look," she said.

He turned. Like everyone who ever saw the setting sun turn the vertical wall of Granite Mountain a bright and glowing pink, he was in awe. "You've got to be kidding me," he said in disbelief as he stood up to get a better look.

But she was not looking at the sunset. She was looking at Spence. His face was crisscrossed with shadow and sunlight, its last pink rays reflecting off his brown hair. And it suddenly occurred to her that of all the beautiful things there were to see in this world—a hidden hot spring, a stunning mountain vista, a multihued sunset—there was nothing in the world so beautiful as a beautiful boy. And she felt sure that, if she lived a hundred years, she would never see anything more beautiful than Spence Markham as he was at this moment.

And then as fast as it came, the moment was gone. The sun disappeared over the horizon, Granite Mountain faded back to granite gray, and Spence was just Spence again. Sweet and smart and simple Spence. Spence whose job it was to take care of her, Spence who would never let her down.

He turned to her. "I think that was the most beautiful thing I've ever seen in my life," he said.

She suddenly became aware that she was staring at him dumbly, and hoped the growing darkness hid whatever hopeless look was plastered to her face.

He reached down for her hand and pulled her into standing position. "Your hands are shaking," he said.

"Oh, sorry," she said, trying to sound normal. "I'm just a little cold all of a sudden."

"You don't have to apologize for being cold," he said, taking off his flannel shirt. "Here, wear this. It'll keep you warm."

He slipped his shirt over her shoulders and she inserted her short arms into its massive sleeves as far as they would go, which was about up to the elbows. As she rolled up the sleeves, Spence climbed up the five-foot step he had helped her down from earlier, got down on his knees, and slipped his hands under Laura's armpits.

"You ready?" he said.

"Ready," she said.

There were no footholds to steady herself on— Spence was responsible for pulling all one hundred pounds of her up the five-foot step all by himself. When she was about midway up, he slid one arm down and wrapped it around her waist to finish with one long, labored pull.

"There's no way this is proper rock-climbing technique," he said once she was finally standing next to him.

"No, it isn't," she said, finding herself too flustered to come up with a more clever reply.

They started the uphill climb. When they got to the first steep incline, Spence grabbed her hand to help her up. They got past the incline. But he didn't let go of her hand. And she didn't let go of his, not even as they started back down the mountain. Fingers intertwined, they continued their journey back to North Powell in silence.

The hike back took about an hour, and she felt mildly delirious the entire time. But once out of the woods and back among the streetlights and ambient noise of North Powell, she was back on earth, and it seemed like that moment with Spence watching the sunset was a thousand years ago. She let go of his hand, and a few minutes later they were walking down her street.

He walked with her up her porch steps. Awkwardly, they stood outside the door.

"Thank you for walking me home," she said.

"No problem," he said. "Thank you for taking me to the hot springs."

Formal thank-yous out of the way, they continued to face one another, each waiting for the other to speak.

Spence took the lead. "Now that I've seen the hot springs for myself, I definitely understand why you wanted to keep it a secret."

"Yeah," she said. "It's pretty great, isn't it?"

"It is."

More silence followed. But this time, she was the one to break it.

"Listen, Spence," she said, "I'm sorry I didn't tell you about the hot springs earlier. It wasn't you I was trying to hide it from—I trust you and David and James completely, you know that. But if word got out to your coworkers and they accidentally let it slip to one of your mega-rich clients–"

"I won't tell anyone but James and David," he said. "And I'll tell them to keep quiet. You can trust them."

She sighed, relieved. "Well, thanks again," she said, turning the key in her door. "You're coming back next Monday, right?"

"Of course," he said. "But I'll call you before then. Give you a status update."

"Great." She opened the door. "Well . . . I guess I'll see you next week, then."

He nodded his head. "I guess you will."

"Goodnight, Spence."

"Goodnight, Laura."

She closed the door. In the darkness, she walked over to the front window and peeked out the curtain, hoping to capture a few last moments with him by watching him walk away. But instead of spotting him on the sidewalk, heading back to Maple Street and his car, she saw him standing on her porch, his forearm pressed against the front door, and his forehead resting upon his arm.

It was then that the realization hit her, swift and hard and a little terrifying: he was standing outside her door because he wanted to stay. And she was watching him from the window because she didn't want him to leave.

She took a sudden step backwards, away from Spence, and away from herself. It took her a few moments to digest the implications of what was going on. Once she had, she cautiously—and curiously—returned to the window and peeked through the curtain.

But there was no one on the porch. The street was empty. Spence was gone.

She walked into her bedroom without turning on the light. It wasn't until she started undressing that she realized she'd forgotten to give Spence his flannel shirt back. Too late now.

She took off his shirt and threw it onto the bed, then unzipped her dress and let it fall on the floor. In nothing but a pair of panties, she dug through her top drawer looking for something to wear as pajamas. She pulled out an old white T-shirt and started to put in on. But then she stopped, flinging it back into the dresser.

Grabbing the sides of her panties, she pulled them off. Naked, she picked up Spence's flannel shirt, put her arms through the sleeves and pulled it tight against her skin. It was warm against her bare breasts and soft against her bare hips.

Naked but for Spence's shirt, she lay down on the bed, grabbed the rolled-up cuffs in her fists, and brought her hands to her face. It smelled like him.

She had a feeling she wasn't going to get much sleep tonight. Over and over again, she found herself returning to the same thought. It was something David had said way back on their very first date, just a few simple words that she'd completely forgotten until tonight.

Spence already went and told everyone that you were really pretty.

Over and over, her mind kept returning to that image of Spence standing in the fading sunlight, staring at the sunset as the shadows from the wispy clouds overhead crisscrossed his face. She didn't know how it was possible that she had never noticed it before. But now that she had, she couldn't get the thought out of her brain.

He was really pretty, too.

CHAPTER 11

It had been an unseasonably warm November thus far, but tonight, just outside the kitchen window, Laura could see a few stray snowflakes falling as she washed the last dinner dish.

Her mom and David were at the kitchen table, finishing their after-dinner coffees.

"I've got to tell you," David said as he sipped at his coffee, "when Laura said she was making Brussels sprouts sautéed with mushrooms over a bed of—what was it?"

"Quinoa," her mom said.

"Over a bed of quinoa, I was terrified. But I can't believe how good that was. So, are you a full-fledged vegetarian yet?"

"Not quite," her mom said. "It's a lot of work trying to make sure you get enough protein without eating any meat. But I've been trying out a lot of new recipes, and of course my princess here is learning to cook vegetarian for her pain-in-the-neck mother."

"You're not a pain in the neck," Laura said as she sat back down at the table. "You cooked for me for eighteen years. I'm just glad I get to cook you a healthy meal once a week."

Her mom leaned over and gave Laura a sideways hug. "You're the best daughter in the world."

"And you're the best mom in the world," Laura said, hugging back.

"I'm still here," David interjected.

Her mom stretched an arm past Laura to bring David into the hugfest. "And I'm so glad Laura found you," she said. "I'll probably destroy your relationship by saying this, but you're the kind of young man every mother dreams of for her daughter."

"You know I welcome and value your opinion, Mom," Laura said. "Especially on men."

Her mom turned to David. "Have we embarrassed you enough for one night, David?" she said. "Or did you want us to argue over who loves the other more? Maybe blow a few kisses back and forth across the table?"

David laughed. "Admittedly, I do feel like I've wandered onto the set of a 1950s sitcom every time I'm with the two of you. And to answer your question, yes, you've embarrassed me enough for one night."

"You're welcome," her mom said. "Walk me home?"

"You're leaving already?" Laura said. "I was going to make that rice pudding you told me about."

"I need to get to bed early tonight," her mom said. "I'm serving at the eight o'clock service tomorrow so I have to be at church by six thirty."

David stood up. "Do you need me to pick anything up on the way back?" he asked Laura as he brought her mom her jacket.

"I think I have everything," Laura said. "I'm going to look up the recipe my mom mentioned. If I need anything, I'll text you. I'm stealing your laptop, by the way."

But David wasn't listening. He was already in the entryway, putting on his coat.

"So are you looking forward to your trip to Austin?" she could hear her mom ask.

"Akron," David said. "And of course I'm looking forward to it. You know, it's more than just the rubber capital of America. It's also the gateway to West Akron."

Her mom giggled. "When do you leave?"

"Monday morning," he said. "A whole week. I can't wait."

The door closed. They were gone.

Laura sat down at the table and opened David's laptop to search for the rice pudding recipe. She'd try to find a vegetarian substitute for turkey while she was at it. Pulling up a browser, she typed "Re" into the address bar. But instead of pulling up Recipes.com, Realestate.com automatically populated.

She was just about to type the correct address into the URL when something caught her eye.

Based on your recent search, we found these homes for you!

Curious, she scrolled down. The first home was a three-bedroom, two-bath in North Powell. The next was a four-bedroom, three-bath with an attached garage. The third was a two-bedroom, one-bath duplex in Bainbridge with no yard or garage but "ample parking on the street." One point two million dollars.

She heard a creak and slapped the laptop shut, fearing it was David about to catch her spying on his browsing history.

But it was just the wind. She returned her focus to the laptop screen, processing the very unexpected discovery she had just made and trying to remain level-headed.

David was looking at family-sized homes in North Powell and Bainbridge. Which didn't necessarily mean anything. As a female of the species, she knew that the fact that you were shopping didn't necessarily mean you had any actual intention of buying. David could have been looking at properties out of a general curiosity about the town his girlfriend lived in. Or maybe to research North Powell demographics for marketing purposes. And the internet in general was known for using the word "recent" very loosely. "Recent search" could mean four months ago.

But then again, it could also mean six weeks ago. As in roughly the night she and Spence had hiked to the hot springs, the night she spent wide-awake in bed with Spence's shirt wrapped around her naked body, rubbing the soft flannel over her breasts and imagining it was Spence's hands.

Stop.

She was doing it. Again. She hadn't felt it for weeks now, and not feeling it had taken extraordinary effort and willpower on her part. She told herself Spence's sudden and overwhelming allure had been a fleeting thing, the temporary result of an evening that any healthy red-blooded female would find romantic. The water was warm, the sunset was beautiful, and the moon was full. The man at her side was strong and protective and sweet and lovely.

He gave her his shirt. He held her hand.

And when she came home that night, Laura Delaney was a little bit in love with Spence Markham.

She'd worked hard to suppress the feeling, and by the following Sunday night she was sure she'd shaken it. But the minute Spence walked through the front door of Powell House Monday morning, the feeling returned, and it was swift and strong and unrelenting. She wanted to be back at the springs. She wanted to be sitting beside him watching the sunset. She wanted him to give her his shirt.

And so it was the next week, and the week after that, and then again the next week, each Monday feeling an attraction to him that she spent the rest of the week fighting off, until little by little, she finally got it under control.

Or so she thought. But here it was again.

She forced Spence out of her mind and David into it. While the initial thrill of their romance had worn off, an ever-deepening bond had taken its place. They weren't able to be together as often as they wished, but when they were together, they were inseparable. They talked and texted every day, and he usually slept over on Wednesday nights. On weekends they basically lived together. Her mom adored him, and the three of them sat together at church every Sunday morning. He was almost family. Spence was just a severe crush. There was no comparison.

She heard the doorknob turning, and immediately typed in "Recipes.com." She was just pulling up the rice pudding recipe when David walked into the kitchen.

"Nice walk home?" she said.

"Very nice," he said. "Your mom wants us to come over when I get back from my dream trip to Akron. She has a meatless lasagna recipe she wants to try."

Laura walked over to the refrigerator and grabbed the milk. "So," she said, "given that you have dinner with my mom on a regular basis and you have her in your phone contacts as 'Mom,' when do I finally get to meet your mother?"

"Never."

"I have to meet her sometime."

"You're a strong and independent woman, Laura," David said, rubbing her shoulders. "You don't have to do anything you don't want to do."

She measured out a teaspoon of allspice. "I want to."

"Let me rephrase that," David said. "You're a strong and independent woman and you don't have to do anything *I* don't want you to do."

She turned to him. "I know you love your mother, David. What makes you think Mom and I won't love her, too?"

"It's not that," he said. "My mom's a very nice person. Really. But she's . . ."

"She's what?"

David heaved a deep sigh. "You know how tonight at dinner with your mom we talked about Teddy Roosevelt and trustbusting?"

"Yeah?"

"And you know how last week we talked about the similarities between Vincent Van Gogh and Edvard Munch?"

"Yes, David, I was there for both those conversations."

"Do you want to know what my mother and I have talked about at dinner the last two Sunday nights?"

Laura ventured a guess. "Winston Churchill's impact on the modern Middle East?"

"Constipation medication. You wouldn't believe how many varieties there are. There are the little red pills, but they take about four days to kick in and then give you diarrhea, and there are the big brown vitamins, but you have to take six of them a day and they're hard to swallow. And then there's the powder you put in your coffee. The powder's the most expensive. But the good news is that the sixty-four-ounce container is on sale this week for only nineteen dollars and ninety-nine cents. I know that because my mother made me go to Walmart last Sunday and buy a lifetime supply before the price went back up to twenty-four dollars."

Laura crossed her arms in front of her chest. "My mother sells life insurance and I teach knitting and sewing. Trust me, about eighty percent of the people we work with have gastrointestinal issues."

"It's not the gastro issues that are the problem," David said. "The problem is that she'll talk about them *at the dinner table*. I love my mother, Laura, but frankly she's not exactly what you'd call a riveting conversationalist."

"I think we can handle it."

"And I think I can't," he said. "Let me sum this up for you, Laura. Your mother is charming and intellectual and funny and beautiful and my mother is constipated. I know your mom wants us both to come for Christmas, but I know it will end with your mom sitting at one end of the table talking about the demise of literature in the twenty-first century and my mom sitting at the other end talking about the different varieties of butter available at the Super Target."

"My mom spends her days talking to complete strangers about their own deaths. She's extremely tactful and can make conversation with anyone."

"Well," David said, "if there's one thing my mother loves more than butter, it's life insurance."

"And my mother loves butter," she said. "She never uses shortening in any of her baking. Does your mother like to bake?"

"No, but she does love to eat."

"There you go," Laura said. "We've got a conversation. Death and pound cake."

"Was that Dostoyevsky or Chekhov? I can never keep my Russian authors straight."

She gave him a teasing slap on the behind. "Dessert will be ready in fifteen minutes," she said. "Go change into something more comfortable. I'll give you a backrub."

David went into the bedroom and Laura went to the stove and poured the milk into the pot. She added the precooked rice and stirred for about five minutes at medium heat, just like the recipe said. Just as she was about to measure out a half-cup of sugar, she felt two hands reach up from behind her and unbutton the top button of her shirt.

"Well," she said as David's lips pressed against the side of her neck. "Aren't we feeling sexy all of a sudden."

"I don't know what's come over me," David said. "There's just something about a naked woman standing in front of a hot stove that really turns me on."

Laura stirred in her spices. "I don't see a naked woman in front of a hot stove."

"You're sure about that?" David said, working his way down to the second button.

"Do you want a nice Indian dessert or not?"

"I want a nice Irish girl first," he said as his hands grabbed her breasts with unusual ferocity.

The next thing she knew, her shirt was being pulled over her head, and before it even hit the floor, her bra was tumbling off her shoulders. A split second later both her skirt and panties were being pulled down her thighs and dropping to the ground.

And just like that, she was a naked woman standing in front of a hot stove. And how she got that way was very, very exciting. Whatever lingering thoughts she had of Spence evaporated, and her mind was fully focused on David and his very skilled hands.

He reached past her and turned off the burner, then brought his hands back to her breasts. She closed her eyes and let the back of her head rest against his shoulder.

"How do you do that?" she said.

"Do what?" he said, nibbling her earlobe.

"Get me so excited so fast."

He squeezed her nipples between his fingers. She reached back to try to return his touch, but in this position all she could do was grab his hips over his jeans. She couldn't even unlatch his belt.

But she liked it like this. Whatever primal urge made the whole big-strong-man thing so sexy was kicking in full force. She loved it that this gorgeous six-foot-tall man could sneak silently into the kitchen and have her completely naked in thirty seconds. She loved how, pressed together like this, his big hands had access to any part of her naked body that he wanted to caress or squeeze or explore. And she liked the element of surprise. She decided to keep her eyes closed so that she wouldn't know what was coming next.

Pulling her tight against him, he reached down with one hand and grabbed her between the legs. She could feel his heart beating rapidly against her back as one finger began massaging her back and forth.

She turned her head to the side, offering up her lips. "David," she said, "kiss me."

He leaned his head down, but in this position, his lips could not reach hers. So he used his firm grip between her legs to lift her whole body up so that her legs were dangling above the ground and her head was dropping back onto his shoulder. He kissed her, hard. And squeezed her, hard.

"Oh God," she heard herself saying.

"Do you like that?" he said.

"I love that," she said. "Don't stop."

Again, he kissed her. Again, he squeezed her. Over and over, kissing, squeezing, massaging.

He jerked her up a little higher so that his mouth could reach her ear. "Tell me what you want," he said.

It was a loaded question. What *didn't* she want?

She found herself indulging. "I want you to do whatever you want to do," she said. "I want you to do things I'm not expecting or imagining." She lowered her voice to a whisper. "This naked body belongs to you, David. I'm all yours."

He stopped squeezing. Gently, he stroked her with his fingertip a few more times.

He was thinking. And she was waiting.

Her body jerked slightly as he tightened his grip between her legs and began carrying her toward the living room. She had no idea what was coming next.

She felt herself being seated face-forward on his lap, the back of her head still resting on his shoulder. He was still fully dressed but she could feel his erection pressed against her backside. She waited to feel what was coming next. And waited.

He was teasing her. They had only been having sex for about three months now, but he had quickly figured out a surefire way to drive her out of her mind: keep her waiting.

She felt the brush of his hands under her thighs. Slowly, he pulled her legs upward so that her knees approached the height of her shoulders. Then, gripping her just under her knees, he pulled her legs apart just slightly.

"Say it again," he said.

"This naked body belongs to you, David," she repeated. "Anything you want."

The word "want" had barely crossed her lips when she heard him let out a stilted breath and simultaneously felt her legs being suddenly pulled open wide. Her arms fell to her sides as her whole body fell limp with surrender. That intense feeling of longing she'd had when David first stripped her naked in the kitchen returned tenfold. With him holding her like this, naked and pliant in his arms, his strong hands holding her legs open, she felt blissfully exposed.

"Can I ask for just one thing?" she said.

"Yes," he said.

"Take your time," she said. "Keep holding me like this. Keep teasing me. Make this last as long as it possibly can, till I want you so bad I can't stand it anymore."

She felt his fingers crawling, spiderlike, down her inner thighs. When they reached the warmth of her, she felt her chest heave in eager anticipation of being caressed and penetrated by his fingers.

But then he dragged his fingertips back up to gently caress the undersides of her knees. She expected them to crawl back down, but instead he slid his hands up her calves to her ankles. Slowly, seductively, he pulled her legs open further. Again she heard herself moaning in anticipation. Every time she felt her legs being pulled open, she instantly wanted to feel him inside her. It was a visceral reaction that she had absolutely no control over. She wanted this to last and last, but she didn't know how much longer she could keep waiting and waiting.

But he wasn't done, and his teasing was about to become merciless.

He positioned her sideways on his lap. His hand between her shoulder blades, he lowered her onto her back over the arm of the chair. She felt a pull in the inner muscle of her thigh as he maneuvered her ankle over his head and rested it on his shoulder. Then he pushed her other leg down so that it lay flat upon his thighs.

The voyeur in him was bringing out the exhibitionist in her, and she felt herself getting even more excited under the weight of his stare. The realization that he was taking such pleasure in watching her shudder at his touch had her so wet that she could feel herself dripping.

"David," she said. "Don't make me wait any longer."

He complied, slipping a finger deep inside her.

"Two fingers," she said.

She felt another finger going in and cried out with pleasure.

He pulled out. "Does that hurt?" he said, alarmed.

"No," she said, panting. "It's good. Keep doing it."

He complied. In went his two big fingers.

"More," she said.

She felt a third finger.

"Good?" he asked as he began moving in and out.

"So good," she said. "I can feel you everywhere. Keep going." But as she was speaking the words, he pulled out entirely. He was up to something.

She felt his fingertips caressing her where she was most wet. She waited to be penetrated again, but instead she felt his fingers exploring her on the outside. She had told him to tease her until she couldn't stand it anymore. He was managing his assignment a little too expertly. He was merciless. It was wonderful.

And then suddenly all three fingers were sinking deep inside her again, and again she cried out in intense pleasure. As before, he began moving his fingers in and out. Again, she had that feeling of being filled to the brim.

Suddenly, he had both her thighs firmly in his grip, and in a single, swift motion, her lower body was being pulled upward. She felt his head between her legs, her head and shoulders dangling upside down over the chair. Her arms hung limply at her sides, and she could feel the carpet brushing up against her knuckles as his mouth bore down on her.

His tongue, usually a gentle tickler, thrust into her. His hands slid down her body and grabbed her breasts. He was now pleasuring all of the most erogenous parts of her body at the same time. As she hung there, straddled upside down over the length of his body, something suddenly occurred to her. She had told him he could do anything he wanted. The possibilities were endless, but of all the choices that fell under the broad heading of "anything," he had chosen to focus on her. Everything he had done in the last half-hour was about pleasing her. He had undressed and caressed her, tickled and teased her, squeezed her and licked her and sucked her and penetrated her. She was being given the thrill ride of her life, and he hadn't so much as taken off his socks.

"David," she said breathlessly from her upside-down position, "I said you could do anything. But everything you've done, you've done for me. Let me give you what you want. Tell me what you want."

He removed his mouth from her just long enough to say, "This is what I want."

Then his tongue was back to work. But she wiggled away. She'd had her turn and now all she wanted to do was please him. She let her hips slide down to his waist and her legs fall down over the two sides of the chair.

"Help me up," she said, breathless.

He grabbed her upper arms and pulled her forward. Straddled over his waist, she was still too exhausted from pleasure to hold herself upright. He wrapped his arms around her back to support her, and he pulled her up against him. Her head fell onto his shoulder.

"There has to be more," she said, her arms hanging limply at her sides. "You've done everything for me. Tell me what you want, I'll do it. I want to do for you what you're doing for me."

He caressed her back with one hand. "That first time I saw you, when you were lying in the back seat of the car, I remember thinking that the only thing that could make your body more beautiful was a man's hands on it. I spent the whole meeting picturing you naked and my hands all over that gorgeous skin. I wanted to make love to you and watch you being made love to at the same time. This is what I've wanted from the beginning. I'm getting exactly what I want."

She felt her energy coming back. She leaned in for a kiss. "David," she said, her lips upon his, "don't you want to watch me sucking you?"

He took a deep breath. "Yes," he said. "Yes, I do."

She pulled back and put her hands on either side of his face. "Then let's get you naked."

He began unbuttoning his shirt as she unzipped his pants. As he stood up and threw his shirt to the floor, she dropped to her knees in front of him and pulled down his pants and boxers. She was about to grab his erection when he pulled her up by the armpits. Once again, she had no idea what he was up to. She closed her eyes again and waited for whatever surprise was next as he carried her several steps forward, then lowered her onto her back.

She could feel the living room carpet beneath her body. He had her in classic missionary position—on her back, arms above her head. Inserting a couch pillow under her head, he pushed her legs into the open position. So much for oral sex. He obviously couldn't wait any longer.

But then came the next surprise. His knees nudged at her armpits, and then he lifted her mouth up to his erection. She kissed him, and with what little mobility she had, ran her lips over his skin before letting her mouth fall open.

It gave her a particular thrill to know that he was looking down and seeing her open lips waiting for him. He pulled her head slightly forward and inserted himself deep into her mouth. Her tongue and lips swallowed him up, and she began sucking as he pushed in. It was a delicate position, and he was gentle in his thrusting. But her response was anything but demure. Open legs automatically triggered her desire to be penetrated, and this position was yet another wonderful tease. It was a very direct cause and effect relationship—

every thrust into her mouth caused an instant stimulation between her legs.

He suddenly pulled out, and she heard him shifting above her. Her arms still extended above her head, she felt his fingers intertwine with hers.

She let her lips fall open again, and once again he began thrusting in deep, long strokes. She had asked him to do things she wasn't expecting or imagining. And in none of her fantasies had she ever imagined this—him hovering above her in missionary posture, making love to her mouth. With every deep thrust in, she felt an intense tingling. She could hear him moaning with pleasure every time she sucked down on him, and her hips instinctively wanted to push upward. But with his calves pinning her thighs, she was completely immobile. All she could do to maximize her pleasure was suck him harder. He was not objecting. His pace increased. So did her tremors.

She had to make a quick decision. Her desire to orgasm with him inside her mouth was intense, but this was supposed to be about him, and he said he wanted to watch himself making love to her. She couldn't orgasm now.

She stopped sucking. He stopped thrusting and pulled out.

"I can't wait any longer," she said.

Breathless, he got himself into standing position. She was so exhausted and short of breath she could barely move, but managed to roll herself over onto her stomach and prop herself up on her hands and knees. "Just give me a sec—"

But there was no second to be had. His arm was around her waist and he was lifting her off the carpet. He held her as he had before, pressed front to back, his hand between her dangling legs.

A moment later, she felt her breasts pressing down against the smooth, hard service of the dining room table. She grabbed its edges for support as David grabbed her hips and leveraged them up. And then he thrust into her with a deep, hard plunge.

She cried out in pleasure. He had never taken her from behind before, and whenever she'd fantasized about it, her knees or feet were always grounded so she could move in sync with his thrusts. But with him holding her hips above the table, she once again found herself completely immobile, and being on the receiving end of David's efforts was giving her a brand-new pleasure. Her hips unmoving, she could feel the full depth and force of his thrusts like never before.

After only a few minutes, her tremors began. From the satisfied moan he let out, she could tell he could feel her walls clenching down on him. His pace increased. She let out a sharp cry.

She lost her grip on the sides of the table and didn't even try to regain it. There was no point. She let her arms hang over the edges while David kept a tight grip on her hips, all the while continuing his forceful thrusts. She gasped for breath as she felt her orgasm approaching. A tremor, another tremor, and then all at once an intense, prolonged spasm. From the deep, broken inhale she heard from behind her, she could tell he was feeling the full force of her climax bearing down on him.

A deep, guttural moan emerged from his throat as he climaxed. A moment later, he collapsed on top of her.

They remained bent over the table together while their racing hearts subsided.

"David?" she said, still a little breathless.

"Hmm?" he said.

"Wow."

Still on top of her, his chest heaved deeply. "Yeah," he concurred. "Wow."

CHAPTER 12

It was another late-day meeting at Powell House. On a normal Monday, Laura would be spending her afternoon thinking loving thoughts about David, preemptively distracting herself from romantic thoughts of Spence. But as of two o'clock, she had no interest in Spence. Or David. Or the Dickens Festival, even though it was now less than three weeks away.

Curled up on her side on her twin mattress, she looked toward the ceiling. She could see just a snippet of the ancient graffito behind the peeling wallpaper . . . *apdoodle*. She wanted to cry, and not just because Grover Cleveland sucked in bed.

The day had started well enough. She'd awoken to find a note from David on her pillow, telling her how much he would miss her while he was in Akron and promising to bring her back a bouquet of rubber chips. She'd spent the next hour in bed, fondly reminiscing about Saturday night's absolutely spectacular sex. She'd then done something she hadn't done in months—taken a solitary hike down one of her favorite paths.

But at two o'clock, she had arrived at Powell House to find her second letter of the day. And this one wasn't nearly as nice as the one from David.

It was from the landmark committee. Her and Spence's request to landmark Powell House had been denied. They wouldn't be getting any grants. Their Powell House adventure was over. She had texted Spence the bad news about an hour ago, but he hadn't texted back. Either he was driving and hadn't read it yet, or he had read it and didn't know how to respond.

She heard the distinctive sound of the front door being pushed open. Then the steps creaking. Then the upstairs hallway floorboards creaking. Then the rusted hinges on her warped bedroom door squeaking. Spence walked in quietly and sat down beside her on the mattress.

"Hey," he said.

She did not respond.

He tugged at her hair. "We did everything we could."

He'd read the text. She grabbed the folded-up letter beside her head and handed it to him. He opened it and read it aloud. "'Dear Dr. and Mrs. Spencer: Your request to have your home landmarked has been denied. Sincerely . . .'" He turned the page over to see if there was perhaps a signature somewhere on the back. "Touching. When did it arrive?"

"The envelope was dated Friday," she said. "Priority overnight delivery."

"They spent twenty-five dollars in postage to tell us no?"

"I guess it's their way of apologizing for not even bothering to sign their names."

"It's strategic," he said, handing her back the letter. "That way we won't know who to call if we want to appeal. How much money is left in the restoration account?"

"Negative six dollars and seventy-three cents. It was twenty-nine dollars and seventy-three cents but the bank charged us thirty-five dollars for being broke."

Rolling onto her back, she closed her eyes and pressed her palms to her forehead, a habit she had picked up from Spence. "I need to get out of here," she said. "Can we work from my house tonight?"

"Sure," he said.

She stood up to leave. But he remained sitting on the mattress.

"Aren't you coming?" she asked.

He grabbed her hand and pulled her back down. "I want to ask you something first."

He was looking unusually serious, and she was a little nervous. "What?" she said.

"Why is this house so important to you?"

She shrugged. "I don't know," she said. "There's no reason, really."

He stayed put. It was clear he wasn't going to budge until he got an explanation.

"Fine," she said. "There's a reason. There's a whole damned story. But I can't tell it without violin music playing in the background, so maybe we should wait until we're in an elevator somewhere."

He didn't push her. But he still didn't budge.

She lay back on the mattress. "If I humiliate myself by getting all melodramatic, you have to promise to audibly sing 'The Band Played On' in its entirety. Deal?"

He gave her a thumbs-up.

She laughed a little at his refusal to speak. "Have it your way," she said. "The story is that my parents tried to buy this place. Back in the day. My mom said that even when they were kids, my dad used to tell my mom how someday he'd buy this house and fix it up all beautiful for her." She cast her eyes downward so she wouldn't have to make eye contact with Spence for the next part. There was no real way to downplay the coming drama, but at least she wouldn't have to see the reaction of pity on his face.

"So anyway," she continued, trying to sound nonchalant, "they grow up, they get married, and one day Mrs. Powell decides she's too old to take care of the place so she puts it on the market. My parents put in an offer, they get approved for a mortgage, lifelong dream come true, blah blah blah. Three days later my mom and I come home from the grocery store and my father's dead on the floor from a brain aneurysm."

He inhaled sharply, which was roughly the reaction she expected. She'd never told him the cause of death before. Or that she'd been there to witness it.

"Don't worry," she said, still looking downward. "I don't remember any of it. Anyhow, the punch line is that my father was twenty-seven when he died. Same age I am now. Same age I was in February when I found out I was in charge of the very house my dad always dreamt of buying for my mom."

She stopped talking, giving Spence a chance to offer some input. But he said nothing.

"I know the age thing is just a stupid coincidence," she said, needing to fill the silent void. "It's not like I think this was destiny or anything. I just kind of felt like it was an opportunity to pick up where my father left off. And when I started stripping the floors, scraping paint, doing all the things he always wanted to do but never got the chance—I finally felt close to him." She kept her eyes down, feeling a little embarrassed. "It was like the work I was doing, we were doing together. Or something stupid like that."

Spence stayed quiet. This was why she hated talking about her father's death. It wasn't so much the story itself. It was people's reaction to it.

She heard a slight shuffle, and then felt him lying down at her side. There was a moment of silence. And then she heard his voice.

"Casey would waltz with the strawberry blonde," he started.

He paused mid-song, nudging her with his elbow, and she couldn't help but giggle a little at his silliness. "I wasn't going to hold you to that," she said.

"I always keep my promises," he said. "I told you that a long time ago."

He nudged her again, and this time she joined in.

Casey would waltz with the strawberry blonde
And the band played on
He'd glide 'cross the floor with the girl he adored
And the band played on
But his brain was so loaded it nearly exploded
The poor girl would shake with alarm
He'd ne'er leave the girl with the strawberry curls
And the band played on.

151

She grew peaceful. "Will I embarrass you again if I say you have a really nice sing—o*w!*" she said as she felt a strong pull on her hair.

"What?" he said innocently. "I was just twirling one of your strawberry curls. No need to shake with alarm."

She teasingly elbowed him.

"Fine," he said, sitting up. "I'll ne'er do it again." He took both her hands and pulled her into sitting position. "Listen," he said, becoming more serious. "Just because we didn't get the landmark status doesn't mean game over. I'll figure something else out. Just give me some time."

"Spence—"

"You can trust me, Laura," he said. "I'm a doctor."

She appreciated his attempt to lighten the mood. But jokes and teasings aside, the rejection from the landmark committee was going to sting for a while. "I know you'll figure something out, Spence," she said. "You always do. But I think right now—can we just talk about something else?"

"Sure," he said. "Is there something specific you wanted to talk about?"

She took a deep breath, emboldening herself. "Yeah," she said. "Commercialized hot springs."

He was taken aback. "You want to talk about commercialization? Now?"

"No," she said. "I want to talk about it never. But I think I need to start getting a grip on reality and since I've already had such a heavy dose of it today, I'm thinking I may as well just pile it all on at once." She looked down at her lap, feeling guilty. "Don't tell anyone this, but I've been wondering if I should drive down to Haven one of these nights after work and see for myself what commercialized hot springs look like."

"Really?" he said.

"Really," she said.

"You said you want to get out of here, right?"

"Like you can't believe."

"Then let's get out of here," he said, standing up. "You have a bathing suit?"

"Yeah," she said.

"Why don't we drive by your house and grab it? I'll call Haven Hot Springs and tell them to hold a room for us."

"You can do that?"

He pulled his wallet out of his back pocket. "They were very happy with the work David and James and I did on their grand opening," he said, pulling out a silver card with his name on it. "They gave us all free lifetime memberships."

She felt guilty just holding a Haven Hot Springs and Spas card in her hand. It was like having the corner pharmacist who'd been filling your family's prescriptions for thirty years catch you walking out of the new chain drugstore with an Rx bag. She was on the verge of betraying the entire town of North Powell by bathing in the enemy. She stood up, handing Spence back his card. "This has to be our little secret, okay?" she said.

"My lips are sealed," he said, putting the card back in his wallet. "Come on, let's go before you change your mind."

Ten minutes later, she was closing the front door of her house and climbing into the passenger seat of Spence's Jeep with a beach tote slung over her shoulder. "Don't you need a bathing suit?" she asked.

"I have one in my gym bag," he said as he pulled out into the street.

She started having second thoughts by the time they reached the Main Street intersection. "Maybe this was a bad idea."

"Too late, I already booked a room," he said, eyeing the road ahead of him. "This will be good for you. Get your mind off of Powell House for a little while."

Less than thirty minutes later, they were pulling into the parking lot of the Haven Hot Springs and Spas.

"It's a miracle," Spence said as he pulled his fifteen-year-old Jeep into a space between a Mercedes and a BMW just yards away from the entrance. "I usually have to park on the street. Careful opening the door," he continued. "If we scratch the car next to you, it will cost five thousand dollars."

"What happens if they scratch your car?"

"Nothing," he said. "My car's only worth twenty bucks."

They inched open their respective car doors and slid themselves out, careful not to breathe on the cars next to them.

"Ready for the tour?" he said.

"Not really," she said. "Can we just get this over with?"

They walked through the gates. Before her eyes were seven large and lavishly designed blue water pools that immediately made her think "Vegas."

"This?" she said, staring at the vast playground of wealth and wonderment in front of her eyes. "You want to do *this* in North Powell?"

"No," he said. "It would be much simpler. Think of this scaled down about ninety percent."

She tried to picture it scaled down ninety percent. It still felt too rich for her blood.

"It's not that bad when you're away from all this nonsense," he said, reading her thoughts as they walked across the spectacle that was the outer playground of the Haven Hot Springs. "I got us a private room. It'll just be the two of us and we can talk about commercialization in peace. We'll get some cucumber water—"

"Some *what*?"

"It's a thing, and you'll be happy you have it once you're in the tub. I can order you a hundred-dollar glass of champagne if you prefer—"

"I'll take the eggplant water."

"Close enough. Come on," he said, nodding toward the door to the private tubs. "You'll like it, you'll see."

Once again, she reluctantly conceded, and Spence used his super-shiny silver membership card to open the door. As he did, she stood on her tiptoes and whispered in his ear. "No offense, Spence, but you seem way out of place here."

He leaned down to her and whispered back. "You have no idea how sorry they are that they gave me this lifetime membership."

Quietly, they both laughed.

They reached the changing rooms. "So you go in that door on the left to change," Spence explained. "Then walk through the door at the far end of the locker room and head down the hallway." He handed her a key fob. "We're in Room 3."

"Okay," she said. She grabbed the knob of the dressing room door, but then stopped. "Listen, Spence," she said as a rush of Irish embarrassment rose in her face. "Um . . . someone bought me my bathing suit as a gift. It's the only one I have."

He studied her, clearly confused as to why she felt compelled to share this fact. "I think most people only have one bathing suit," he said, trying to be understanding.

"The point is that it was a gift," she repeated. "I didn't pick it out myself."

"Okay," he said, still clueless. "Thanks for letting me know?"

She nodded, and they entered their respective changing rooms. She slipped off her clothes and began awkwardly changing into the bathing suit David had bought for her the day they'd first made love. It was also the last time she'd worn the bathing suit, and she was beginning to remember why. It took five minutes to get it on right. But when at long last she did, she slung her towel over her forearm and exited the changing room.

The hallway was very dim, lit only by decorative electric candles behind glass panes built into the walls. Some kind of weird—but thankfully soft—meditative music played from invisible speakers. Room 3 was the second on the left.

After several tries with the key fob, she succeeded in opening the door.

He was sitting in the hot tub. His eyes were closed, his head hanging back in a position of extreme relaxation. A glass of cucumber water was on the ledge behind him. It was clear that he hadn't heard her come in.

She'd never seen him without a shirt on before. He had broad shoulders and a long, lean torso—well developed, but not with that ridiculous sculpted look of a man who spent way too much time at the gym. He had hair on his chest, like a real man. One look at his very healthy arms had her flashing back to that night at the North Powell springs, how he had grabbed her by the hips and lifted her down the steep drop with ease.

And once again, the feeling was back. But now it came with a new twist. That night at the North Powell hot springs, he became pretty. Tonight, at Haven, he officially became hot. And it wasn't just because he looked nice shirtless. It was because of the way she was looking at him. He looked, quite simply, like a man. And not just any man—the kind of man who could make you very glad you were a woman.

She looked at the tub. Instead of the standard round model with a bench, it was about triple the size and crafted to look like springs found in nature, amorphous and surrounded by real rocks. In addition to rock benches, there were long flat rocks to lie on. It was a smaller, indoor version of the North Powell hot springs. And it was lovely.

She walked to the steps of the tub. "Hey, Spence," she said quietly.

He lifted his head and opened his eyes. His glance moved just slightly, first down the length of her body, then up again, and then back to her face. He was looking at her the way she had just been looking at him.

"Hey . . ." he said. "Hey, Laura."

"Sorry I took so long. I couldn't figure out how to get this key fob thing to work."

He said nothing.

"Where do I put my towel?" she said.

"Just leave it on the floor," he said.

She dropped her towel on the floor, then pulled the scrunchie out of her hair and tossed it aside.

"Now what?" she said.

Spence smiled a little at her awkwardness. "It's the same as an outside hot spring. You come in."

She put her foot on the first step of the tub. Then the second. Then the third, until she was standing about mid-thigh in the water. She'd never been a big fan of regular poolside tubs—they were always way too hot. But the Haven tub was different. The temperature was exactly right, like a warm bath.

Two more steps and she was in, the water up to her waist. Scooping up some water in her hands, she poured it down her arms. "It feels different from the water in the North Powell springs," she said. "It's . . . soft or something."

"It's the minerals," he said.

She poured some more handfuls down her arms. "It's nice," she said.

"I told you."

"So, what do I do now?"

He stood up. "C'mere, girl," he said, taking her hand and pulling her into the middle of the tub. "Turn around."

"Why?" she said.

Taking her by the shoulders, he gently turned her around so that she was facing the door. Then he placed both of his hands on the small of her back. "Lie back," he said.

She leaned back against his chest as he lifted her up.

And suddenly she got what all the fuss was about. She was floating. But not normal floating. Like the salt in the Dead Sea, the soft minerals in the water raised her body up so effortlessly that it was more like floating on a cloud than on water.

His hands slid up her back just a few inches, until her shoulders were resting in the crook of his elbows. He began walking backwards, slowly. And the ride began. Her back, her hips, and her thighs rose above the water, and the soft mineral waves that lapped over her stomach felt like soft fingertips caressing her skin. As her long hair spread out in a fan around her head, she let the water lift her arms out to her sides, and she could feel the edges of Spence's hands just barely grazing the undersides of her breasts as he pulled her around the hot tub in long, lazy circles.

"Do you like it?" she heard Spence say quietly.

Not opening her eyes, she nodded.

A few more slow laps, and the ride ended. Without letting go of her, he sat down and pulled her in close, so that she lay sideways above his lap. Beneath her, the gentle waves continued to roll.

"Um," he said, hesitant. "Did you want to talk about commercial devel—"

"No."

She could just barely hear his voice as he whispered back. "Me neither."

He wrapped an arm around her, cradling her against his chest, his other hand holding her at the waist. And so they remained, her floating silently in his arms, him embracing her, for who knew how long, well over an hour. He was making her feel the way she felt that night at the North Powell hot springs—protected, peaceful, safe. But this time it was giving him a devastating sex appeal. Who knew safe could be so sexy?

She felt two light fingertips press softly upon her lips. For a moment they just rested there, unmoving. She let her mouth open just slightly, and felt Spence's fingers moving slowly back and forth across her lower lip, then trace her entire mouth.

And then his touch was gone. She heard the faintest splash of water, and then a handful of water was being poured over her head. With his right arm still holding her close against his chest, his left hand smoothed back her wet hair. Over and over, water dripping over her head, then Spence's hand smoothing back her hair. Sometimes the water would trickle forward, down her nose and over her opened lips, and she would feel the slightest burn of minerals in her throat before Spence began tracing her mouth with his fingers again.

"Spence?" she said, eyes still closed.

"Hmm?"

"Can I have some water?"

She expected to feel the glass being placed in her hand. But instead she felt it being pressed against her lower lip. He tilted the glass and poured, and she could feel the soothing cool water hit the back of her throat. He lowered the glass.

He let her head slip back down into the crook of his shoulder, and she let her mouth open in anticipation of more water dripping over her lips. But this time he poured handfuls of water over her shoulders. She could feel the soft water run down her arms, or sometimes meander sideways to the crease of her neck and down between her breasts. Handful after handful of warm water ran over her.

She opened her eyes and looked up at him. His eyes did not meet hers. They were looking down at her breasts. She could see him watching as the water snaked itself over her curves and into her cleavage. He repeated this, over and over, not seeming to tire of the view. At last, he looked at her face and saw her looking up at him from within the safe snuggle of his arms. He placed his fingers on her lips once more.

"Hey, girl," he said quietly.

She reached her hand up to his face, running her fingers down his cheek and letting her thumb caress his lower lip. "Hey, boy."

Knock knock knock.

"Excuse me, Mr. Markham," said a voice outside the door.

He dropped his head forward, and she could see him mouth the word *no*. He reluctantly lifted his head back up. "Yes?" he called to the voice outside the door.

"The showers close in fifteen minutes. Spa closes in twenty."

Suddenly the lights came on, bright.

"Thank you," he called, then looked down at Laura with a hopeless smile. "Rude awakening."

"Yeah," she said. For the first time in almost two hours, she pulled herself upright. It felt strange to be back on her feet. "I think it's going to take me a few minutes to get my land legs back," she said, climbing out of the tub. She grabbed her towel off the floor. "Are you coming?"

"In a minute," he said. "Go ahead and grab a quick shower. I'll meet you at the entrance."

"Okay," she said.

She opened the door and walked into the hallway. She was pretty sure the last two hours had been about the best of her life, but she was only three paces outside the door before she was struck by an overwhelming guilt.

David. How long had they been together now? Almost six months. She tried to let herself off the hook by telling herself that they'd never made an official commitment. But it was no use. Two nights ago the words "inseparable" and "family" had been going through her mind. That hadn't changed in the last forty-eight hours.

She and Spence hadn't even kissed, but there was no denying that the way they'd spent the last two hours went way beyond the boundaries of friendship. This was absolutely a betrayal of David's trust, and if the shoe were on the other foot, she would consider it enough of a reason to end the relationship.

She showered quickly and changed back into day clothes. When she emerged from the private spas building, Spence was waiting for her right outside.

"Hey," she said, reverting to her previous just-friends demeanor, careful to keep a safe two feet away from him.

"Hey," he said. "Did you want to grab a coffee or anything?"

"Oh, no thanks," she said casually. "It's late. I think I'd just like to get home."

It suddenly occurred to her that she might not know Spence as well as she thought she did. What if he took her "I think I'd just like to get home," as "I think I'd just like to get home so we can rip off each other's clothes and jump into bed"? She didn't think he was the type, and he should know her well enough by now to know *she* wasn't—but nonetheless, it was better to play it safe.

"You were right, the springs really are relaxing," she said. "I have a feeling I'm going to fall asleep in the entryway as soon as I walk through the front door."

The look on his face told her that he got the point.

"Yeah," he said. "Yeah, me too."

He looked disappointed, and she felt a double wave of guilt. She had managed to betray David and mislead Spence in a single trip to a hot tub. As she and Spence climbed into his Jeep, it occurred to her that it was going to be a very long night for both of them. He would be thinking of her. And she would be doing

163

everything in her power to push any and all thoughts of him out of her mind.

"Should be a quick ride home," he said. "No traffic this time of night."

"Yeah," she said.

It turned out to be an extremely long ride home, at least on an interpersonal level. They said nothing to one another the entire ride.

"We're here," he said, pulling up in front of her house.

"Thanks for taking me to Haven," she said. "You were right. It's really nice."

"I'm glad you liked it," he said.

He usually walked her to her front door, but she hopped out before he had a chance to exit his Jeep and open her car door for her. "Well, thanks again," she said, trying to get away as quickly as possible. "Drive safe."

She held it together as she walked up the steps. But as soon as she walked in the darkened house and heard Spence drive away, she flopped down cross-legged onto the floor and buried her face in her hands. She wanted to be lying next to David in a warm bed, kissing him and telling him there was no one else but him. The problem was, she wanted to be doing the exact same thing with Spence.

She had shaken off her feelings for Spence once before. But she wasn't sure she could do it again. That night after their hike, she hadn't known for sure whether it was just a one-night thing, a purely physical and fleeting attraction. And more importantly, she hadn't known if Spence felt that way back.

But after tonight, there was no doubt. Spence felt that way. And she felt that way. And it wasn't just physical.

What the hell was she going to do?

CHAPTER 13

Laura we really need to finalize the plans for Dickens can I come by tomorrow afternoon

It was one thirty the following Wednesday afternoon, and Laura sat cross-legged on her sales counter reading yesterday's text conversation with Spence.

Good idea. 2pm?

sounds good see you tomorrow

It was now tomorrow, and she was nervous. He'd never come to North Powell on a Wednesday before. Was it because he actually wanted to finalize Dickens? Or was it because he couldn't wait until next Monday to see her, even after all the awkwardness of two nights ago?

The bell above her front door jingled. Spence walked in, closing the door behind him.

He was wearing a baseball cap, and his hands were inserted into his pockets. If she had to describe him in one word, it would be "self-conscious." But maybe she was imagining it. She hoped she was.

"Hey, Laura," he said, coming to the counter. "How's your week going?"

"Busy," she said. "You?"

"Busy."

There was a silence that was, as expected, awkward. She decided to be the one to break it. "So," she said, opening her laptop, "Dickens. Where should we—"

"Can we talk?" he said, interrupting. "About Monday night? Can we please get that out of the way first?"

She pushed her laptop to the side. "Yeah," she said. "You're right. Let's get that out of the way."

"Okay," he began, his hands still in his pockets. "I'll start. The office is constantly getting on my case about my unprofessional manner, and I don't know, maybe they're right. Monday night . . . I think I just— you said you wanted to see the hot springs, and a private room cost three hundred dollars an hour and I knew I could get you in for free, so all I was thinking was to take you there so you could see it for yourself. I swear that's all I meant it to be. But then you walked into the room in that bathing suit and . . ."

He stopped, bringing his hands to his temples and making the hand sign people make to say "mind blown."

She said nothing. But her palpitating heart was speaking volumes.

"I know I crossed a line, Laura, and I'm sorry, but I want you to know that before Monday night I never even thought of you that way. I mean—maybe I did. Once or twice. The time you were laying tiles in those denim shorts . . . anyway, whatever, I should probably just stop talking now—"

"It's okay," she said quickly. "I understand. I never thought of you that way before either. But then I walked into the room and saw you sitting there in the hot tub and—" She stopped mid-sentence, bringing her hands up and mimicking his "mind blown" gesture. "You didn't do anything wrong, Spence. Everything we did, we did together."

"No," he said, "I was the one who told you to lay down on my arms. I was the one with my hands all over your body all night and not the other way around."

"And I was the one who didn't stop you for two hours. I was there because I wanted to be, Spence. Everything you did—I wanted it, okay? You have no idea how badly I wanted it. If that stupid manager hadn't kicked us out . . ."

She trailed off. She couldn't say what she was thinking. *If that stupid manager hadn't kicked us out, you would have kissed me. And I wouldn't have stopped you.*

"Listen, it happened," Spence said. "For what it's worth, you looked nice. You felt nice. I work all the time and I don't really meet women so I guess I just . . . whatever. It happened. But it was a one-time thing and I just want you to know that I think we make a good team professionally, and hope we can keep working together without letting this one-time thing get in the way."

But it was too late. With nothing more than a verbal reminder of his hands "all over her body," the "one-time thing" was already very much in the way. The same maddening desire she'd felt at Haven was sweeping over her again. He looked at her a certain way, and just like that, he was *such a man*. A man who liked cradling a woman's head against his chest and watching the soft waves of a hot spring cascade over her stomach. A man who liked the feeling of a woman sighing in his arms as the warm water he poured over her lips snaked itself down her neck and over the curve of her breasts into her cleavage. He was a man, and he could be driven to distraction by desire. He was a man, he was a man, he was a man. And he was very, very good at it.

The words he had said at their first meeting echoed through her head, albeit in a wildly different context.

I'm all yours, Laura.

She wanted him, all of him, all to herself. His mouth bearing down on hers, her breasts pressed against his chest, his naked body on top of hers.

You belong to me.

She wanted to give her whole body to him, to give every inch of her skin over, to satisfy him in every way a woman could possibly satisfy a man.

C'mere, girl.

C'mere, boy.

"So," she heard him say, interrupting her thoughts, "are we good?"

She didn't move or look him in the face. She just needed to take a few moments to get the images in her head under control before she dare lay eyes on Spence. But try as she might to focus, she could not silence her brain, nor could she stop the longing pulsating deep inside her. The nice girl whose mother taught her that a lady never swears wanted nothing more than to lay her mouth on Spence Markham's ear and tenderly whisper those two little words every man wants to hear.

Fuck me.

Her brain was screaming it so loud that for a moment she was worried she actually said it.

"Yeah," she thankfully heard herself say instead, "we're good."

"Okay then," he said. "Do you want to go back to the sewing room and put the finishing touches on the festival plans?"

"I do," she said, hopping off the counter.

They walked back to the sewing room and got down to actual marketing work for the first time in about two months. Spence steered his focus to his laptop. And Laura tried to keep her focus on one thing and one thing only.

David. David. David.

CHAPTER 14

She felt like she hadn't stopped moving all day. Next week was Thanksgiving and Spence would be away the whole week visiting family, so she would be on her own this coming Monday. But the festival was less than a few short weeks away, and there were still about a million little details that had to be ironed out.

But she wouldn't be ironing out any festival details tonight. It was Friday. David had just returned from Akron this afternoon and they hadn't even spoken since last Sunday. She wanted tonight to be extra special, not just because they hadn't seen each other for almost a week. She wanted to make up for what she'd done Monday night with Spence. The fact that David didn't know about it didn't matter.

A grocery bag in one arm, she stuck her key in the lock, only to find that the front door was already open. The only people who had keys to her house were her mom, Spence, and David. It obviously wasn't David—he probably hadn't even left the city yet. It definitely wasn't Spence. Cautiously, she opened the door.

"Mom?" she called. "Is that you?"

But when she entered the kitchen, it was David she found. He was leaning against the counter, arms crossed in front of his chest. His posture was casual, but he looked very tense. He did not say hello.

She slipped off her shoes and walked over to the counter. "Hey," she said, putting her bags down. "I wasn't expecting you so early. How long have you been here?"

"Can I ask you a favor?" he said. He did not sound happy.

She had a feeling she knew where this was going. "Sure," she said, turning to unpack a grocery bag.

"In the future, can you please not climb half-naked into any hot tubs with Spence Markham while I'm conveniently away on a business trip?"

Crap. Crap, crap, *crap*.

She put some cans in the cabinet. "I'm sorry," she said.

"Sorry for what?" he said.

"I'm just sorry. You're mad at me, right?"

"You said you were sorry, which means you think you have something to be sorry for. I'd like to hear from you what that something is."

She finally turned around to face him. "I shouldn't have gone hot-tubbing with Spence. It was a lapse of judgment. On my part."

"Lapse in judgement?" he repeated, unimpressed. "Would you like hear about the great conversation I had with Spence today when I went to his office this afternoon to get an update on the campaign?"

She would not. "Sure."

"'Hey Spence, has Laura brought up the idea of developing the hot springs since that first time?' 'Funny you should mention it, David, on Monday she said she wanted to see what a commercialized hot spring looked like so I took her to Haven.' 'Oh? How'd she like it?' 'She loved it, David. Once we got in the tub, she didn't want to leave. After about two hours the manager finally had to kick us out.' 'Us?' I say. 'Yeah,' he says. 'Us.' 'Just curious,' I say, 'what was she wearing?' 'A black bikini with purple lace,' he tells me. 'With a bow that untied at the cleavage.' 'Sounds pretty sexy,' I say, 'I hope you enjoyed the view.' 'As a matter of fact it was pretty sexy and I did enjoy the view,' he says. And do you want to hear what he says to me next?"

"I don't think so."

"He wants to know what the hell *my* problem is."

"He doesn't even know about us, so you can't blame him. We just went there for business, and—"

"Maybe it was just business for you. But I've known Markham since he was twenty-one and just so you know, we've exchanged a little guy talk over the years and I happen to know he's what you might call a 'breast man.' So trust me, we can take his word for it when he says he was enjoying the view."

"*You* used the words *enjoying the view*. He was just repeating what you said."

"Thank you for coming to his defense. I really appreciate that sentiment right now."

"I didn't mean it like that."

"He could have just said you were wearing a bathing suit. But no, he made special mention of the fact that your bikini top untied at the cleavage, which he obviously spent a lot of time thinking about. And I've seen you in that bikini, so you can trust me on this one, there is *no way in hell* Spence Markham's mind was on business while you were sitting next to him in a hot tub wearing the black push-up bikini I bought for you. For my eyes only, remember? 'Not suitable for public use.' Those were your words, not mine."

"It was the only bathing suit I had," Laura said.

"And what was he wearing?"

"I don't know," she said, starting to become frustrated. "He never got out of the water."

"He never got out of the water," David repeated. "And that didn't raise any suspicion?"

"Why would that raise any suspicion? He was in the water when I got in, and I left first."

David closed his eyes and shook his head incredulously. "He had a hard-on, okay, Laura? My male coworker had a hard-on for my girlfriend while I was fourteen hundred miles away on business, and that's why he never got out of the water in front of you."

If she wasn't in love with Spence before, she was now. "*For two hours?*"

"Curb your enthusiasm," David said. "It was probably off and on. But I promise you that's the reason he waited until you were out of the room before he got out of the tub."

She stayed silent. There was nothing she could say that wouldn't make it worse. The fact was that she and Spence had done a hell of a lot more than sit next to each other in that hot tub. And incidentally, business hadn't been on her mind, either. And oh, by the way, she'd already figured out that he was a "breast man" on her own. And also she'd kinda had a crush on him since that evening she'd held his hand in the woods and then come home and rubbed his shirt all over her naked body for about six hours straight. And oh, yeah, she thought the words "fuck me" when she saw him two days ago, but the good news was that she was about eighty percent sure she didn't say it out loud.

She approached David, gently laying a hand on his chest. "I'm sorry," she said. "It was a very bad call. On my part. Be mad at me all you want. But please, don't blame this on Spence. He doesn't even know about us."

"Yeah, he does."

"No, he doesn't. I never told him."

"I did."

She froze.

"Spence and I had a very nice chat before I came here and I made it very clear to him what my relationship with you is and what his relationship with you is not."

She was afraid to ask the next question. "And what did he say?"

David walked over to the table and sat down. "He said he was sorry. He said he had no idea we were a couple and he'd never move in on my girlfriend and promised it wouldn't happen again."

"And what did you say?"

He dropped his head in his hands. "I said thanks."

In an unexpected flair of emotion, Laura felt herself becoming angry. "Well," she said, sitting down across from him, "I'm glad you and Spence got your little property war sorted out. From now on I'll be sure to wear my dog tag everywhere I go so other men will know who my owner is."

"I didn't use the word 'property,' you did."

"No, David, you didn't. Just like you've never said the words 'commitment' or 'exclusive.' Ever. Hell, David, up until one minute ago I've never even heard you use the word 'girlfriend' in reference to me."

He looked at her from across the table, unimpressed. "I never used the words 'commitment' and 'girlfriend'? Seriously? That's your argument?"

"Yes, David, that's my argument."

"Well, how about this, Laura? I use the words 'I love you' every time I see you. I say it *every time* I get off the phone with you, and I say it every time we make love."

She looked down at the table, ashamed.

"We buy groceries together, Laura," he continued. "We wash dishes and do laundry together. We go to church together and then we have lunch with your mom, who incidentally has asked me to start calling her 'Mom.' Everything we do is a *we*. What are *we* doing this weekend? *We* need to buy new sheets for *our* bed. But you know what, you're right. *We* as a couple never made any kind of commitment. But just so you know, *I* did. I have been committed to you since our first goddamned kiss and I haven't so much as looked at another woman since the moment I saw your feet dangling out of your goddamned car window. So here's my question for you. Are *you* committed to *me*? Because at the moment you seem more committed to semantics than you do to our relationship."

She stood up, not even able to meet his eyes. When you're right, you're right, and David was completely right. Walking over to his side of the table, she straddled his lap and wrapped her arms around his back before laying her head on his shoulder. A little hesitantly, he placed his hands on her waist.

"I'm sorry," she said. "I know you love me. And not just because you say it. You show it. I feel it. You're a good person and you're good to me and you make me happy. And it *is* a commitment on my part. You're the best thing that's happened to me in a long time and I'm lucky to have you. You can be mad at me if you want, but I hope you'll forgive me."

She could feel his shoulders relaxing a little.

"I'm not mad at you," he said. "I'm overreacting. It's a hot tub, not a bed. You didn't do anything. It's . . . "

He left his sentence hanging.

"It's what?" Laura asked.

"It's Markham, okay? It's not you, it's him. He spends every single Monday with you, which is more time than he's spent with any other client *ever*. Trust me, people have noticed. I didn't want to have to tell you this, but . . . "

He pulled his phone out and began scrolling through his texts. "This isn't your fault, okay? And I apologize in advance that some of the guys at KPS have no concept of what constitutes appropriate workplace behavior. I'm not trying to hurt you or embarrass you, I'm just doing this to show you what I'm dealing with back at the office. This is from over a month ago."

He handed her the phone. She read the text.

> *Hey David we're taking a poll. So is Markham fucking this chick in North Powell or what? Remember, your vote counts.*

It was followed by a wink emoji. David took the phone from her hand and scrolled to another text.

"Here," he said, "this one's my favorite. I asked one of the guys in Creative Services if he knew where Markham was. This was his response."

He held up the text for Laura to see.

> *Probably in North Powell getting his weekly blowjob.*

"Oh my God," she said, looking away. "That's awful. And it's . . . awful. Oh my God."

"It's not always that offensive," he said, this time checking his emails. "This one's from Karen in reception. She's a grandmother."

He handed his phone to her.

> *Does anyone have Spence's girlfriend's home address? I have to send her a package but Spence said to send it to her house not the store. I think maybe it's their anniversary or something.*

David took his phone back. "You have no idea how much it sucks to sit there and read a mass email to every single person in the company referring to you as 'Spence's girlfriend' and not being able to say a damned thing about it. I liked the blowjob text better. What the hell was he sending to your house anyway?"

She rubbed her forehead, which suddenly hurt. "Doorknobs," she said.

"*Doorknobs?*"

"Glass doorknobs for Powell House. They're antiques, his father found them at an estate sale and—whatever, David. I'm so, so sorry you have to deal with this. I had no idea. Please tell me Spence doesn't know about these texts."

"Don't worry, as usual he's completely clueless. Besides, how would he know what people are saying about him around the office? He's always here."

His voice was becoming irritated again. She watched as he visibly calmed himself down, then set his phone facedown on the table.

"I'm sorry," he said. "I'm not mad at you. I'm just mad in general. I know Spence has been helping you with this historic house and I know he's a skilled carpenter and all that, but the last text I got from you said you didn't get your landmark status so there's no reason to keep working on the house, right?"

She nodded, hoping her face wasn't betraying what she was feeling on the inside. She knew what he was about to say.

"And when do you see him next?"

"The Monday after Thanksgiving."

"And then the festival is the following weekend and then that's it, right? There's no reason to see him anymore?"

She shook her head.

"And you understand what I'm saying?"

She nodded again. She understood what he was saying so well it hurt. "You don't want me seeing Spence anymore."

"I don't want Spence seeing you anymore. It's not you, okay? It's him. Remember that. When the marketing campaign is over I'm going to tell KPS that we've started dating. That way I'm not dating a client,

I'm dating a former client. There are no rules against that."

She laid her head on his shoulder. What he was telling her was extremely painful. But oddly enough, she felt a tiny bit of relief. Her feelings for Spence were genuine, but out of sight, out of mind, wasn't that the expression? If she stopped seeing him, she would stop feeling for him. Eventually. It wouldn't be overnight, and it wouldn't be easy. But if she had to choose—and she did—she chose David.

She leancd up for a kiss. "I do love you, David," she said.

At last, he wrapped his arms tightly around her. And kissed her. She felt loved, and she felt forgiven. She didn't want to violate his trust again.

Pressing the tip of her nose against his, she whispered, "I haven't had sex with a really hot guy in over a week. How about you?"

David caressed her back. "There was this one guy I met on the plane, but he wasn't that hot. I couldn't even remember his name when we woke up the next morning."

She laughed. Since that very first day when he'd asked her to marry him because he'd never have a better "how I met your mom" story, he had displayed a sharp sense of humor. It was sexy then, and it was sexy now. "When was the last time we took a shower together?" she said.

"Not since Tuesday night," he said. "Oh, wait, I'm thinking of the guy from the plane again."

She pulled his shirt over his head. "If you spent less time trying to make me jealous and more time trying to make me naked, you'd be in the shower right now getting a full-service and highly personalized scrub down."

She could tell by the look on his face that he was seeing the validity of her rationale. "Because there appears to be a lot in it for me," he said, "I've decided to let you win this debate."

He stood up, lifted her into his arms and carried her toward the bathroom. It was time for the make-up festivities to begin.

CHAPTER 15

do you need me tomorrow or can you get by without me

It was the Sunday after Thanksgiving, just five days before the first day of the festival. The one-sentence text from Spence arrived at 11:45 p.m. Which meant he was probably lying in bed when he wrote it. Thinking about her, unable to sleep. Debating what he should do and concluding it was for the best that he not come to see her tomorrow.

From the loneliness of her own bed, she began typing.

I always need you, Spence. I have no idea how I'll get by without you. But I promised David that

She backspaced and started over.

I was lying when I said that Haven was the first time I thought of you that way. I think about you that way all the time.

She backspaced over that one, too. And thus began a long string of texts, each of which she erased, and most of which had nothing to do with his question.

*I've relived that night in Haven in my mind a
million times. It felt so good to be in your arms
and I didn't want it to end. Were you going to
kiss me? I wish you had kissed me.*

Backspace. Start again.

*The only thing I need from you is your for-
giveness. You're the sweetest thing in my life,
Spence, and I can't bear to think of life without
you.*

She liked that one. It captured exactly what she was
feeling. And told Spence everything she wanted him to
know.

But she backspaced over that one, too. She had no
business thinking about or feeling anything towards
anyone but David. She didn't realize how much she
loved him until she saw how much her behavior had
hurt him. And if David knew how well-founded his
suspicions about her and Spence were, he would have
been even more hurt. His request that she not see
Spence once the festival was over was more reasonable
than he knew. She might have an out-of-control crush
on Spence, but David was the man she loved. He was
kind and loving and crazy-devoted to her and she
wanted to be the woman he deserved.

She composed a new text.

I need you, Spence. But I'll get by without you.

She hit send.

If Spence chose to read between the lines, he would
understand what she was saying. *I need you, Spence. I*

might be in love with you. But I can't have you both.
And I choose him.

She waited for his response. And waited. Every few minutes she'd see a string of dots appear, indicating that Spence was composing a text, but then it would stop, indicating that he was playing the backspacing game, too. Write something meaningful. Delete. Spill his heart. Delete. Tell her he needed her, too. Delete.

Finally, at 12:40 a.m., her text tone pinged.

Ok see you friday night at the festival

It took him forty-five minutes worth of false starts to come back with that response. He had read between the lines. The relationship they never had was over, and the love story of Spence and Laura would always be an unfinished book. Would he have kissed her if he could have? If he had kissed her, would the ending have changed? Would she have chosen him instead?

She picked up her phone and composed one last text.

I wish you had kissed me that night at Haven.

She hesitated for just a moment, and then hit send. Opening the top drawer of her nightstand, she stuck her phone in and then stuffed some clothes on top of it to muffle any sound. She then crawled over to the other side of the bed—David's side. This was their room, this was the bed they shared. No matter how stressful or awful or miserable the world outside was, here in their bed he should always feel safe. He should always be able to curl up under the covers with the woman who loved him and know that she was always on his side, no matter what.

She pulled Spence's flannel shirt off her shoulders and threw it on the floor. Reaching into David's nightstand, she pulled out one of his T-shirts and put it on instead, then laid her head on his pillow and curled up in his half of the blanket.

From a few feet away, she could just barely hear a ping. She pulled the blanket up over her head, telling herself that she was imagining it. But her text tone was set to ping twice for every text, and when she heard it again, there was no doubt that it was real.

She slid back over to her side of the bed. She put her hand on the drawer handle, hesitating. Just because she had received a text didn't mean she had to read it.

But who was she kidding? She yanked open the drawer.

It was from Spence. It was the shortest text he had ever sent her, just two words.

me too

CHAPTER 16

As the sun began its descent on the late afternoon of Friday, December 3rd, Laura and her mom stood on the sidewalk outside of Creations. Main Street was clear of cars, as were the three blocks of the Victorian district. For the next three nights, Main, Maple, Chestnut and Oak were designated no-parking streets.

Three horse-drawn carriages and their drivers were parked in front of St. Martin's, ready to transport children to Santa's workshop on Oak Street. Every storefront was decorated to the hilt, and every Victorian streetlamp had a sprig of mistletoe hanging from it. The shop and restaurant owners were already dressed in their Dickensian garb, and slowly—a little too slowly—the tourists were starting to arrive. So far there were all of three families wandering up and down the street, but none were in Victorian clothing. At least the little girls had princess dresses on.

"David's going to be so proud of you," her mom said, wrapping an arm around her nervous daughter's shoulder. "He gets back from Finland tomorrow, right?"

"Amsterdam," Laura said. "And he gets back Sunday morning. He's coming straight to the festival from the airport."

"Do you want me to send him some pictures of Main Street before the crowd gets here?"

"I already sent him about three hundred."

"What'd he think?"

"I don't know yet," Laura said. "It's something like 2 a.m. in Amsterdam, so he'll see them when he wakes up and how come there are only three families here, Mom? What if this whole festival is a total train wreck and I'm the one who engineered it all?"

"The festival doesn't officially start for fifteen minutes," her mom reassured her. "David already told us not to expect people until after seven. It's a weeknight and they'll be driving in from the city after work. So stop worrying."

But Laura had to worry. There was much more at stake than her mom realized. If Dickens was a bust, then that was it. North Powell would have no other choice than to start the process of commercializing the hot springs. So Dickens couldn't just be "that one time" someone visited North Powell. It had to be the first of many times they visited North Powell. Getting people to come back again and again was the key to keeping the hot springs, and North Powell itself, pristine. It was the reason Spence had insisted they spend four thousand dollars replacing the tiny and humble "Welcome to North Powell" sign with a colorful eighteen-by-ten-foot billboard that said "Welcome Back." It was also why he had come up with the idea of hanging mistletoe off of every streetlamp—it would put people in the mind for romance and make them want to come back for Valentine's Day. The B and B owners would be handing out their twenty-percent-off romantic getaway fliers for the whole festival, and most of the restaurants were holding nightly raffles for a free Valentine's dinner. Stores likes Laura's were handing out coupons valid only for February thirteenth through fifteenth.

If all went as hoped, visitors would already have made Valentine's reservations by the time they left the Dickens Festival. And in nine weeks from now, when they were checking out of their bed-and-breakfast room on February fifteenth and heading for brunch at one of North Powell's fine dining establishments, they'd already be making plans to bring the whole family back for spring butterflies, summer horseback riding, Jeep tours, and so on and so forth.

"I wonder if we should have planned something for New Year's," Laura said, wondering aloud.

"Hmm?" her mom said.

"David keeps saying how the key to success is to keep the momentum going, but James said that the average consumer's attention span is only three days or something. I'm afraid that by Valentine's Day people will forget we're here, no matter how many coupons and fliers we hand out. So maybe we should have planned something for New Year's."

"Come on," her mom said, "let's go back inside. Time to put on your dress and stop worrying about a future you can't control."

"You're trying to distract me."

"Yes. I am. You've worked night and day on this for months and you couldn't possibly have done more than you have. You've done a great job, and now it's time to stop worrying and start enjoying the fruits of your labor."

As they walked back to the sewing room, Laura realized that her mom's distraction trick was working. Laura had missed prom, which meant she had never actually worn a floor-length dress. She was excited to see the dress that her mom had made just for her.

She closed the door and stripped down to her bra and panties.

"No bra," her mom said.

"Seriously?"

"It's an off-the-shoulder dress. That's what you wanted, right?"

"Yeah," Laura said, unlatching her bra. "I just didn't think you were actually going to do it."

"Arms up."

"You're going to dress me?"

"Yes. Close your eyes."

Standing in her underwear with her eyes closed, Laura heard some rustling behind her as her mom took the dress out from under its plastic cover.

"Can I please dress myself?" Laura said. "This is a little embarrassing."

"No. I never get to surprise you anymore. Just let me have this one."

Laura kept her eyes closed as her mom pulled the dress down over her midsection. "Can I at least put my own boobs into place?" she asked.

"Fine. But keep your eyes closed."

Laura reached into the bust of her dress and reposi-tioned her breasts so they each fit neatly into their proper places, a little ritual that no B-cup woman like her mom would ever understand. She ran her fingers across the bodice, which was surprisingly low-cut.

"Wow, Mom," Laura said. "Letting me show off the twins for a change. Thanks."

"I only did it because you specifically requested it. I believe the wording of your text was 'Okay, you can make my dress but only if you promise to let Terry and Tracy out to have a little fun.'"

"I wrote that?" Laura said. "I didn't realize I was so clever. I—*owww.*"

"You wanted a real Victorian dress. Real Victorian dresses had bustiers. Hold still, I just have to finish adjusting the ties and then you can look."

"I can't breathe. Not so tight."

"Fine," her mom said, loosening the ties that ran up the back of the dress.

"Can I look?"

"Almost."

Laura could feel her mom smoothing out the skirt and puffing up the elbow-length sleeves. She then pulled Laura's long hair behind her shoulders. "Okay, beautiful," she said. "You can open your eyes."

Laura opened her eyes and looked at herself in the mirror.

"Oh my gosh!" she exclaimed. The dress was a pale blue, with a deep neckline that stretched to the corners of each shoulder. From there, the elegant but not-too-puffy sleeves hung down to just above her elbows and tied in simple bows. The bust area was an off-white cotton that gathered at the center with a pull tie and showed off her cleavage very nicely. It was form-fitting down to the hips, at which point the ankle-length skirt flared out just enough to look genuinely Victorian. It was simple but eloquent, subtle but beautiful.

"Wait till David sees you on Sunday," her mom said. "He's going to go nuts."

"I love it, Mom," Laura said. "This is the most beautiful dress I've ever seen."

"Do I get to do your hair?"

"You don't think I should wear it down?"

"I'll tie back the sides so you can still wear it long. We'll let some curls dangle in the front. You'll look like something out of a Charlotte Brontë novel."

Five minutes later, her mom was putting the finishing touches on Laura's hair. "You've never been prettier," she said. "Go put your makeup on. I'll call you later to see how things are going."

"Thank you, Mom," Laura said, wrapping her arms around her mom's waist. "I love my dress."

"Nothing's too good for my baby," her mom said. She gave Laura a big bear hug, and departed.

Getting closer to the mirror, Laura put on a layer of clear lip gloss and just a touch of blush. Her dress and hair were understated, and a heavily made-up face wouldn't fit in with the rest of the picture.

Taking a step back, she took one last look in the mirror. She looked good. And natural. Spence would like her like this. She wondered when he'd get here. She hoped it would be soon.

She hadn't bothered trying to put him out of her mind. Soon he'd be gone forever, and her thoughts of him would be all she had left. Besides, she couldn't get him out of her mind if she'd wanted to. She could be thinking about the history of backgammon or the implications of the freaking helium shortage and somehow her brain would find a way to make it have something to do with Spence. Did backgammon originate in Asia or the Middle East and had Spence ever traveled in Asia? Where the hell is all the helium going and I wonder if Spence ever lost a balloon when he was a little boy? Every road led to Spence.

There was one only thing that would make her thoughts and feelings for him go away—his absence. It would be here soon enough.

A few hours later, the store was packed. She looked over at Nathan, the high school junior she had hired to work the register. After a few false starts, he seemed to have figured it out and was serving a long line of customers.

"Excuse me," said an elderly woman dressed as Miss Havisham. "Is there a store around here where I can buy organics?"

"Of course," Laura said. "John's Apothecary. It's the last store on this side of the street. They make all the soaps and cleansers on premises and host soapmaking workshops every second Saturday."

"Thank you, dear," said Miss Havisham.

"Of course. Be sure to visit our B and Bs. They're all serving free snacks and beverages."

She texted Nathan.

Are you remembering to say "Hope to see you back here for Valentine's Day!" to every customer?

He looked up and gave her a thumbs-up from across the room.

Laura looked back down at her phone. 8:40 p.m. and still no Spence. Either he wasn't here, or he was here and choosing not to come to the store to see her. She bitterly regretted telling him not to come this past Monday. She'd let their last precious hours together slip through her fingers because she was too stupid to say, "Yes, Spence I need you. Yes, Spence, I was wrong, but please don't take our last ten hours together away from me. It's all we have left."

If he didn't come tonight, Sunday was the last time she would see him. Tomorrow he had a cousin's wedding. He would be helping her in the Christmas craft room at St. Martin's on Sunday, but they'd be surrounded by children and lucky if they had time to even wave to one another.

He had to come tonight.

The bell above the door jingled, and Laura whipped her head towards the entrance. It wasn't Spence. It was an attractive thirtysomething couple who, based on their stunning costumes, were no doubt going to walk around her store speaking in very loud and very bad faux-English accents for fifteen minutes before leaving without buying anything with their wads of cash—but *not* before having chased about fifteen people out of the store with their obnoxious fake accents.

The bell rang again. Another neck whip. Another person who was not Spence.

But it was close.

"James!" Laura called out. "Back here!"

Smiling, James walked across the store with a little redheaded girl of about four perched on his hip.

"And who would this princess be?" Laura asked.

"This is Becca," James said. "It's past her bedtime so she's a little grumpy. I have one more around here somewhere. We're going to get going as soon as I find her."

"Bonnie, right?" Laura said. "Nine?"

"No. Bella. Eleven months."

"You lost an eleven-month-old!"

"No, I lost a thirty-one-year-old. She's with Spence. We got separated about twenty minutes ago."

"Oh," Laura said, trying to sound casual. "I didn't realize Spence came tonight."

"Of course he came," James said. "You didn't think he'd miss opening night, did you?"

"Yeah," she said, flustered. "I mean no. I mean, you're right, he's worked so hard on it. I'm sure he wants to see it with his own eyes."

"Well, I've got to tell you, you guys did a great job. Have you been out yet?"

"No, I've been stuck in here all night."

"It's a mob scene out there. People are loving it, and it's just the first night."

"Are people visiting the B and Bs?"

"Oh yeah," he said. "There are more people in the Victorian district than there are on Main Street and— oh, that reminds me, I almost forget the most important thing." He grabbed her arm and pulled her away from the crowd. "Spence has been going door-to-door and he told me to tell you that every single one of the B and Bs said people are already making reservations for Valentine's Day." He lowered his voice to a whisper. "So the hot springs are safe. For now at least."

Laura smiled a nervous smile, hoping James couldn't see how upset she was. She couldn't give less of a crap about the B and Bs and the hot springs. All she cared about was the fact that Spence had come to the festival but was sending her messages via James. That could only mean one thing. He had no intention of coming to the shop and seeing her in person.

"Are you okay?" James asked.

"Me?" she said. "I'm great. It's just this dress. I'm roasting."

He seemed to fall for the ruse. "Tell me about it," he said. "It's December—who thought it was going to be sixty-five degrees out, right? These pants," he said, gesturing to his thick Victorian trousers, "are pure wool. And I think this shirt Bethany dressed me in is made of mohair or something."

"What about Spence?" she said. Speaking of mohair. As usual, all roads led to him. "I assume he's not dressed up?"

"You'll never believe this, but he's not only wearing a black shirt, he's wearing a *new* black shirt. With a collar and everything. And jeans and sneakers, of course."

The bell rang, and Laura laughed nervously as she spied yet another incoming patron who wasn't Spence.

"I guess a new shirt's the best we can expect from a thirty-one-year-old man who doesn't even know how to tie a tie," she said, trying to hide her nerves behind casual conversation.

"Spence?" James said, raising an eyebrow. "Spence knows how to tie a tie. What makes you think he doesn't?"

She felt her jaw drop. "Spence knows how to tie a tie?" she said, almost yelling. "Are you sure?"

She remembered back to that day when they had hand-delivered their application to the landmark committee. That was back in August, three full months before Spence had supposedly first thought about her "that way." Only now she realized that Haven wasn't the first time. This confirmed he'd been thinking about her "that way" since at least mid-August. That's why he kept taking his tie off. So she'd have to keep retying it for him. So he could feel her hands on his neck as she pushed up his collar.

"Wow," James said in response to Laura's excessively strong reaction, "you'd think I'd just told you that he knows how to wrestle an alligator. Yes, believe it or not, my fashion-impaired brother-in-law knows how to tie a tie. He's the one who taught me how to do it. Sophomore year in college. In retrospect, I should have returned the favor and taught him how to buy a new pair of shoes. I remember this one time, junior year I think, that he—"

"Spence," Laura said, darting toward the door.

She could just barely see his head jutting above the large swarm of people walking into her store at once. Like an actual Victorian lady, she pulled her skirt up above her ankles so that she wouldn't trip as she pushed her way through the crowd. As she got closer, she could see a tiny head. It was eleven-month-old Bella, her head resting on Spence's shoulder.

Spence didn't see her until she practically crashed into him.

"Laura," he began. "Are you—oh God," he said, seeing the distressed look on her face.

"I thought you weren't coming," she said.

He wrapped his free arm around her as she buried her face in his shoulder. "I'm sorry," he said. "I didn't know what to do. I wanted to come earlier, I just—I should have come earlier." He pulled her in tighter. "It's okay. I'm here now."

She felt a tug on her hair. She glanced up, expecting to find Spence's finger twirling one of her curls. But instead she saw Bella's tiny hand pulling one of her loose locks.

"Hey, you," Spence said, bouncing Bella in his arm. "What are you trying to do, pull Laura's hair out?"

Bella was just reaching up for Spence's nose when Laura heard an angry voice behind her. "So what's the deal, Spence?" It was James.

"It's complicated," Spence said as James took Bella from him. "Can you please just not mention this to anyone in the office?"

"So the rumors are true?"

"Yes," Spence said defensively.

"Exactly how stupid are you?" James said. "And you," he continued, addressing the back of Laura's head. "You realize he could get fired for this, right? Do you understand the risk you've put him at?"

"Hey, James," Spence snapped. "Remember that time in senior year when my eighteen-year-old sister came to visit me for the weekend and by Sunday afternoon she was pregnant?"

James was suddenly silent.

"I'm pretty sure you still owe me one for lying to my father and telling him you'd been dating my teenaged sister for a year before you knocked her up, so how about you do me a favor and leave Laura out of this? She's upset enough and she didn't do anything wrong."

At that, Spence embraced Laura with both arms, and she could feel his lips pressing down against the top of her head. "I'm here now," he said again in a voice just loud enough for her alone to hear.

The next sound they heard was a little girl crying. "It's okay, Becca," James said, his voice suddenly becoming soothing. "Daddy and Uncle Pants aren't fighting." In a voice not quite as soothing, but at least a little less hostile, he added, "I'm sorry, Laura. I wasn't going to tell on Spence, trust me. I just—"

She unburied her face from Spence's chest just long enough to turn to James and mouth that it was okay.

"We'll talk in the car," James said to Spence.

"Yeah," Spence said.

James departed.

"Do you have someone on the register?" Spence asked.

She sniffled, wiping away a tear. "Yes."

"Come on," he said. "Let's go to the sewing room."

He took her hand and they worked their way through the crowd and into the classroom. The first thing he did after closing the door was take both her hands in his and hold them out so he could take a long look at her in her Victorian dress.

"Wow," he said. "If I'd known you looked this beautiful, I would have been here hours ago." He brought her hands up to his mouth and kissed them. "I'm sorry, Laura."

He sat down on one of the metal chairs. Stepping in close, she took his head in her arms as he embraced her waist. In her low-cut dress, she could feel his soft brown hair brushing up against her breasts.

"Please don't apologize, Spence," she said, stroking his hair. "You've been wonderful from the very beginning. You promised you would take care of me and that's all you've ever done." She laid her lips on the top of his head. "Trusting you was the best decision I ever made."

She could feel his lips against the exposed part of her breast, and heard herself sigh audibly as his mouth worked its way across her bustline, one soft kiss upon her breasts after another.

She stroked his hair with her fingers. "Oh," she sighed, "Spence."

He pulled back and took a deep breath. After a few quiet moments, he spoke. "Sunday night, when we were texting back and forth," he began, "I could see that you were texting me and then stopping. Then texting again and stopping. What were you writing?"

She remembered back to Sunday night. Watching little text dots appear on her screen and then disappear, agonizingly wondering what he kept deleting.

Finally, she spoke the words she had so desperately wanted to write that night. "I was saying that you're the sweetest thing in my life. And I don't know how I'm going to get by without you."

He gave a sigh of relief and pulled her onto his lap. She instantly curled up, allowing herself to be cradled in his arms.

Her head on his shoulder, she closed her eyes. "What were you writing to me?" she whispered.

He gave a forlorn laugh. "A novel, I think. So much I don't even remember everything. Something about how when the campaign's over and I stop coming to North Powell—when I'm stuck back at KPS and in the rat race without you—what then?" He grew silent for a moment. "I was so sure we were going to be together once the campaign ended, you know? I didn't even question it. I thought you felt the same way and that we were just waiting it out for the sake of professionalism."

She tilted her head up to find him looking down at her.

"I was so miserable for such a long time and I've been so happy these last six months," he said. "I don't know how I can ever go back, Laura. I don't know how I'll ever find someone else like you."

She had been expecting him to say something like *I was texting that I wanted to see you again* or a vague *I was telling you how I feel.* Instead she was getting a *What will I do without you. You've made me so happy. I'll never find someone like you.* Her heart was beating so hard and so fast that she could feel a suffocating pulse in her throat.

His text tone pinged. It was the one he set for work. Letting go with one arm, he reluctantly took his phone out of his pocket. He stared at his message for far longer than it took to read it.

"I'm sorry, Laura," he finally said. "I have to go."

He couldn't be serious.

"Why are they calling you now?" she protested. "You're already at work, don't they get that? You're at the festival, it's part of your job to be here."

"It's James," he said. "We all came in his minivan. Bethany has morning sickness and James wants to sit in the back with her, so they need me to drive. I'm really sorry, Laura, she's pregnant with twins this time and gets really sick at night. I can't just leave her—"

Laura took a deep breath, calming herself down. It was just James, not work. And Bethany was feeling sick. "I understand," she said. "We can talk more on Sunday, right?"

He looked away, saying nothing.

"Spence," she said, beginning to panic, "you're going to be here Sunday, right? We're supposed to run the craft room together."

"David's coming back on Sunday morning, right? He's coming straight from the airport?"

"Yes, but—"

"You don't really think he's going to leave us alone together, do you? He's never going to let you out of his sight as long as he thinks I'm anywhere within a hundred yards. He'll be right there next to you in the craft room all day and I'm just going to have to sit there and take it, just like I had to sit there and take it when he told me about the two of you. You can't ask me go through that again, Laura."

He was right. David would be glued to her all day. If she had to sit there and watch Spence with another woman, it would be agony. "You're right, Spence," she said, dejected. "I can't ask you to do that. You shouldn't come on Sunday."

Which meant that this was the end. In five minutes he would be gone. There would no more restless Sunday nights lying awake thinking about him, no more Monday mornings filled with joyful anticipation of the coming day at his side. And tomorrow and Sunday and Monday—and every day for the rest of her life—would be without Spence.

She slid off his lap and sat down on the floor in front of him. Laying her head on his lap, she wrapped her arms around his back. She could feel him stroking her hair. By her calculation, she had roughly four minutes left with him, and they were dwindling fast.

"Laura?" he said.

"Yeah?"

"Are you really going to do this?"

She lifted her head off his lap and looked up at him. "Do what?"

"Let me leave like this? Let me walk out that door and never come back?"

She remained silent.

"I know you want me and you know that I'm yours for the asking. So explain it to me. Why are you acting like you don't have a choice in the matter? You're not married to him. You don't even live together."

She lowered her eyes as she wiped away her first tear. "It's not that easy, Spence," she said.

"Why?"

She looked up at him, hoping she could find the right words to make him understand. "How many people do you have that you'd describe as loved ones? People you can count on to always have your back? People you would do anything for?"

"Including you?" he said.

God, he was making this hard. "I meant family," she said, looking away.

"I don't know," he said. "Two parents, three sisters, three nieces. My brother-in-law. What does this have to do with—"

"David and I have each other," she said. "Aside from our mothers—who aren't going to live forever—that's what we have. Each other. I don't know if someone who hasn't been there can understand it, but when you've spent your whole life with only one or two people to love, you just love them *so, so* much. You'd do anything to protect them. You're only happy if they're happy and it rips your heart out to see them sad. Breakups are hard on anyone, but for people like David or me—you wouldn't believe the hole it leaves in your heart. It's like having a leg chopped off or something."

"Trust me, Laura, I get it," Spence said. "I'm going through that right now."

Every time he spoke, he made it harder.

"Please don't do this, Spence," she said. "There are only three people in this world that I can't stand to see unhappy and you're one of them."

"Laura, I get it that you don't want to see David hurt. Believe it or not, I don't hate him nearly as much as he hates me and I don't want to see him get hurt either. I know he's a good guy. I know his mom's his only relative. But what are you going to do, spend the rest of your life with him because you don't want to hurt him?"

"It's not just that, Spence. I—"

She stopped.

"You what?"

She looked at the ground. She didn't want to have to say it. She didn't want Spence to have to hear it. But he was giving her no choice. "I love him, Spence."

Silence followed. She did not look at him, and she assumed he wasn't looking at her back.

"I guess I can't top that," she heard him quietly say.

He stood. She watched his feet walking toward the door. She saw the door opening, and Spence walking out of it.

And that was it. It was over.

He was gone.

CHAPTER 17

Laura sat cross-legged on her bedroom floor in her Victorian dress, her eyes closed, her back against the wall. It was Sunday, the last day of the festival. She had looked forward to Dickens for six months straight. Now she couldn't wait for it to end.

Saturday had been absolutely awful. Twelve straight hours of sneaking glances at the front door of Creations, remembering the moment on Friday when Spence had come in and welcomed her into his arms like it was the most natural thing in the world—only to turn around and walk out of her life forever thirty minutes later.

She was glad she wasn't going to be working the store today, and would instead be at the church leading crafting activities. In terms of memories, St. Martin's was a Spence-free zone. She had figured out a way to make tonight Spence-free as well. Her overnight bag was packed and ready to go. Since Mondays were her day off again, she would sleep at David's tonight.

The festival ended at six. They'd drive back to his place, and she'd make him salmon pasta with cream sauce, his favorite. In her bag she had packed a brand-new lingerie set that David had never seen her in before.

With him having been away on travel almost constantly recently, they hadn't had sex in two weeks. Tonight was going to be extra special. It was, after all, the first night of the rest of their lives—the night she finally started letting go of Spence and rededicating herself to David.

She felt a kiss on her forehead. The moment she opened her eyes and saw him, her whole being flooded with a sense of peace.

"David," she said, squeezing his hand. "You're home."

He took her other hand and pulled her into standing position. "Wow," he said, looking at her in her Victorian dress. "I feel like I came from the airport and went straight to the prom with the prettiest girl in school. When does craft day start?"

"In a half hour," she said. "As soon as church ends."

"In that case," he said, taking out his phone. She could see him scrolling.

"In that case what?" she said.

He laid his phone down on the dresser and extended one hand to her. "May I?"

She took his hand, having no idea what he was up to. But then the music started. He pulled her into a slow dance position as a melody she didn't recognize began to play.

> *I didn't know which way to go*
> *I saw some footprints in the snow*
> *I followed, I followed.*

I wandered deep into the pines
I saw a light, your hand in mine
I found you, I found you.

She looked up at David as she finally recognized the song she hadn't heard since she was a little girl. "'You Found Me'?" she said. "This was my parents' wedding song."

He leaned in and kissed her on her forehead. "I know," he said. "Your mom told me."

She laid her head on his shoulder as they swayed in a lazy circle. "I didn't go to my prom," she whispered as they slow-danced. "I had the flu. I had to just lie there in bed staring at my prom dress hanging in the closet. I cried all night."

"I know," David said, laying his head on top of hers. "Your mom told me."

He pulled her in closer and began singing along. "I asked you fa la la la la I don't know all the words yet something about the snowflakes in your hair fa la la."

Laura smiled and began singing where he left off. "*I saw some letters in the snow, I kneeled down, I read them slow, I love you, I love you.*"

The music ended, but they didn't let go of one another.

"I bought you something in Amsterdam," David whispered as they embraced in the silence. "Do you want to see it?"

"Mmm," she said, relaxing in his arms.

She felt something tapping her shoulder.

"Open your eyes," he said.

She opened her eyes. In the small space between them was a small burgundy box. He pushed the lid open with his thumb, revealing its contents.

"Oh my God," she gasped.

"Laura Delaney," he said, "will you marry me?"

"Oh my God," she repeated.

"I know it's sudden," David said. "And I know you weren't expecting this, so I'm sorry if—"

She flung both arms tightly around his neck, and he returned her embrace.

"I'm not expecting you to answer right away," he whispered in her ear. "But just so you know, if you'd said yes the first time I proposed to you, I would have skipped the meeting, walked us straight into town hall and married you on the spot."

She remembered back to that first morning, when he'd jokingly asked her to marry him. He'd made her laugh. He'd put her at ease.

She didn't sleep a wink after their first date, when he'd kissed her and said, *Please tell me I don't have to wait a whole week to see you again.* Nor did she sleep the night of their second date, when he'd thanked her for making him so stupidly happy that he hadn't gotten anything done in a week. But they had both slept deeply the night they'd first made love, the night he first told her he loved her. Since then, it had become a given that every free moment was to be spent together. Her bed became their bed. Her room became their room. And now, he was asking that the rest of her life become the rest of their lives.

She didn't know the answer to his question yet. But she knew one thing with absolute certainty. Placing her hands on either side of his face, she whispered, "I love you, David."

They hadn't kissed in weeks. She'd almost forgotten what a good kisser he was.

"I love you, Laura," he said as his lips moved down her neck to her bare shoulders. He ran his fingers across the low-cut bodice of her dress, then tugged on the front string, opening up her full cleavage to him. "God, I missed you," he said as he lowered himself to his knees and pulled her dress down to just below her breasts. She closed her eyes as he took one breast in his mouth, the other in his hand. She hadn't forgotten how good he was with his hands.

Reaching up her skirt, he grabbed the edges of her panties. "Remind me again when the craft room opens?"

"I can be a few minutes late."

"Are you—"

"I'm sure," she said. "Don't stop."

He pulled her panties down her thighs until they were on the floor. As he stood back up, she unbuttoned his pants and pulled down the zipper, inserting both hands into his boxers. He let out a moan.

"Nice?" she said as she stroked him.

"Very nice," he said.

She squeezed tight and he let out another moan. It had been two weeks of abstinence, and he was rock-solid and ready.

Scooping her up, he took her to the bed.

With her back on the bed and her long Victorian skirt pushed up above her hips, she felt almost transported back in time, like she and David were two star-crossed lovers sneaking in a few forbidden moments in the servants' quarters before her father returned from the hunt. The fantasy added an extra touch of sweetness to an already lovely moment.

He grasped her ankles and pulled them up to his shoulders. They only had a few minutes, and his fingertips caressed her just once before she felt him slide in. He began moving in those long, deep thrusts he was so good at. They were technically in a hurry, but she hoped he would take his time. Pacing was everything, and those slow thrusts were the pinnacle of his skill set.

But this time something was different. Along with the usual pleasure, she felt an unusual sense of peace. For the last month, their sex had always been sprinkled with a dash of guilt. There was always another man in the background. But Spence was gone, and this moment was hers and David's alone. He loved her. He wanted to marry her. And there was no one else but him. Making love to him had never been so romantic.

He held her thighs tight against his torso as his pace became more rapid, his thrusts more forceful. She felt her first tremor, and he felt it along with her.

"God, I love it when you do that," he said, his pace increasing even more. Another tremor came, and another moan from David. She relaxed her leg muscles until his pace increased to the point that she knew his orgasm was imminent. When she felt him approaching climax, she clenched her leg muscles again, and her orgasm hit her full-force as he ejaculated and collapsed on top of her.

As she lay beneath him, she caressed his hair. "Sometimes I can't believe how much I love you," she said. "Every time we make love, I feel it."

He remained silent.

"David?" she said. "Sweetie?"

He was asleep.

Jet lag. She'd momentarily forgotten that his body and sleep cycle were eight hours ahead of hers. Furthermore, he'd been working twelve- and fourteen-hour days the whole time he was in Amsterdam. And on top of that, she'd just given him an extra-heavy dose of the most tried-and-true elixir in the history of the sedatives market: great sex. For all she knew, he would be out cold for the next ten hours.

Careful not to wake him, she writhed out from under his body and, with some struggle, lifted his legs onto the bed. After stuffing a pillow snugly under his head and covering him with a blanket, she dug around his pants pockets. When she found his phone, she placed it next to his head. She'd call him in a few hours to wake him. If he slept all day, he'd be awake all night and end up falling asleep in the middle of the workday tomorrow.

She was giving him a kiss on the forehead when she heard her text tone coming from the kitchen, no doubt her mom pinging her to tell her that services had ended and it was time to open the craft room. Quietly closing the bedroom door behind her, she hurried into the kitchen. She picked up her phone, ready to text, "Be there in five."

But the text wasn't from her mom. It was from Spence, and contained only one word.

Laura

There was nothing else. Just *Laura.*
Her heart began pounding. She typed back.

Spence?

She waited about a minute, but there was no response. But there was also no time to sit around waiting. She had five minutes to get to St. Martin's for craft day. She stuck her phone in her bag. She'd check her texts later.

At two o'clock, Laura looked down at her phone. It was officially "later," and Spence still hadn't texted back. She couldn't even imagine a scenario that would have resulted in a text that contained just her name. It was as if she had texted him saying *Hey do you have any idea what my name is I can't remember* and he had sent back *Laura* in response.

Her phone alarm went off. It was time to wake up David.

She dialed his number, but it went to voicemail.

"Dammit," she said, startling the three seven-year-old girls who were sitting on the floor cutting Christmas snowflakes.

"I meant 'darn it,'" she said. She stood up and yelled across the room to her mom. "I'm going to run home and wake David. Are you okay on your own for a little bit?"

"Do you want me to go over and wake him?"

"No," Laura said. "He's expecting me."

Her mom gave her a thumbs-up before returning her attention to the bevy of little boys sitting at her table making clay snowmen.

"You just keep working on your snowflakes," Laura said to the little girls. "If you need anything, ask that lady over there in the polka-dot dress."

The girls returned to their snowflakes, and Laura headed home. As she stepped out of St. Martin's and onto Main Street, she could see the hustle and bustle of the shopping district several blocks ahead. Her own store had broken its own record in single-day receipts, and all reports from the shops, restaurants, and B and B owners indicated that the festival was a monster success.

She turned right onto Sydney, then left onto Quincy, and then up the porch stairs and through her front door.

"David?" she called out.

There was no reply. She walked into the bedroom. His blanket and pillow were on the bed, but he was not.

"David?" she called again.

That was when she saw a note on the bed.

Hey Sweetheart,

So sorry I had to leave early. The new CEO says she wants the Amsterdam report by tomorrow morning (she's a psychopath) so I'm heading back to the office. I'm really sorry I didn't get to see the festival after you worked so hard on it. I know you had plans to come back to the city with me tonight. I promise I'll make it up to you. Remember to lock the door.

Love you, David.

She folded up the note and put it in the drawer of David's nightstand, then lay down on David's side of the bed. She picked up her phone and texted her mom.

> *I'm suddenly exhausted. Would you be able to call Pam or someone and ask them to help you in the craft room? I think I need to rest.*

A few minutes later her mom texted back.

> *I asked Jonelle to help, she's on her way now. Take the rest of the day off. Talk soon.*

She embraced David's pillow in her arms and held it tight. She loved him. He loved her. She made him happy. He made her happy. He wanted to marry her, and there was only one thing standing between them and a lifetime of happiness. And with nothing more than a one-word text—*Laura*—that one thing was making her question whether she could ever marry David back.

CHAPTER 18

Seven hours later, the first annual North Powell Dickens Festival was over. The crowds were gone. The stores were closed. After three straight days of nonstop revelry, the North Powell shopping district was suddenly a ghost town.

Laura walked down Main Street. In her left hand was her overnight bag, and in her right hand was her fold-up camping mattress. Under one arm she carried her blanket and pillow.

She couldn't sleep at home tonight. Everything reminded her of David. She couldn't sleep at Powell House. Everything reminded her of Spence. So she was going to sleep at her store. The storage closet was just big enough for her mattress and—bonus—neither Spence nor David had ever been in it.

She walked into Creations by Laura without turning on the light. She was in a dark mood and wanted to be in a dark place. On tonight's agenda was an intense round of cleaning, and the light filtering into the store from the streetlamp would be sufficient to clean by.

Walking into the storage closet and flicking on the plug-in nightlight, she set up her bed and threw the overnight bag she had packed for David's on top of it. She caught a glimpse of herself in the dusty mirror above the sink. Strands of her long hair were falling out of her scrunchie and spilling messily onto her bare shoulders, the same way it had that night at Haven. As she had so many times before, she returned to the moment when Spence had first looked up to see her standing there in her bikini, and she'd realized he was looking at her *that way*. He'd opened his eyes and seen a woman, soft and curvy, warm-fleshed and waiting. She'd walked through the door and seen a man, big and muscular, touchable, kissable. He'd extended a hand to her, then issued an invitation.

Lie back.

But this time the memory was different. She was seeing it in the third person, watching herself and Spence from above. And there was a twist. She was naked. His hands on her back as she floated on the waves, naked. Being pulled into his embrace, cradled in his protective arms, naked. His palm running up the wet skin of her stomach and onto her breast. A lovely caress, and then suddenly they were in the deep waters of the North Powell hot springs. Spence was standing upright, holding her. His arms were around her waist, and her legs were around his hips. Kissing and caressing, a trickle of warm spring water flowed between their two naked bodies—

She opened her eyes, bringing the fantasy to an abrupt halt. Grabbing her overnight bag, she dug around until she found the lingerie set she'd planned to wear for David tonight. The tag said "Snow Angel," but the only thing snowy about it was that the lacy parts were reminiscent of snowflakes. Otherwise it was pure sexwear, nothing angelic about it.

She took off her sweat suit, sports bra and boy shorts and tossed them onto the shelf. Snipping off the tag with a pair of sewing scissors, she stepped into her Snow Angel panties. The front was a delicate white lace. The back was a demi-thong. The front and the back tied together at the hips with satin strings.

She slipped the baby doll top over her head. It was really nothing more than an off-the-shoulder sheath and was so flimsy it barely even qualified as clothing. Sheer but for the delicate lace along the top and bottom hems, all that held it closed in the front was a single satin tie just above her breasts. She pulled the neckline down over her shoulders so that the elastic clung to her upper arms, and looked at herself in the mirror.

She looked how she felt: sexy and sad. Sexy because she could see her bare breasts through the nightie's sheer fabric and she couldn't forget the way Spence stared at her as the water he poured over her shoulders snaked across her chest and down her cleavage. Sexy because she was sure her lacy white demi-thong would make Spence want her as much as she wanted him.

And sad because she was supposed to be dressed like this for David, but all she could think of was Spence. Her sad, her sexy, her longing, her joy, and, she was starting to believe, her heart—all of it was for Spence. She pulled her phone out of her bag and once again checked her texts. But there was still no follow-up to his cryptic *Laura*.

She felt her lip begin to quiver. She grabbed a bucket and a bottle of cleaning fluid off the shelf as Spence's words from Friday night filled her brain.

I've been so happy. She poured some cleaning fluid into the bucket and left it in the sink to fill with water as she put on her yellow cleaning gloves. *I was so sure we were going to be together.* She pulled a sponge out of the drawer and tossed it into the water bucket. *I'll never find someone like you.*

Once the heavy bucket was full, she grabbed its handle with both hands and lugged it into the store, heading to a darkened corner. Then she got down on her knees, pulled out the huge cleaning sponge, and began scrubbing forward and back, forward and back.

But it was no use. After only a minute, she tossed the sponge in the bucket and pulled off her gloves. Spence was gone. He was really gone. And he was gone because she had let him go, so sure that David was the one that she'd never even given herself the chance to ponder the possibility that it was Spence she was meant to be with.

But now she was rethinking her choices. Not because Spence had told her that he'd never find anyone else like her. Not because of the longing that had swept over her when he laid his lips on her breasts or the comfort she'd felt as he stroked her hair while she cried into his lap.

Rather, it was a brief moment she'd barely noted at the time. She'd awoken with it on her mind Saturday morning, and by bedtime, the memory of it was rocking her to sleep like a love song.

Then this morning, David had made her forget for a little while, when he asked her to spend the rest of her life with him and they made love for the first time in weeks. But afterwards, she had walked into a craft room full of giggling children, and by noon she was so distracted that she couldn't think straight. And since then, she felt like she had been able to think about one thing and one thing only: how very, very nice Spence looked holding that baby.

It couldn't have lasted more than thirty seconds. He'd held Laura in one arm and baby Bella in the other. *It's okay, I'm here now*, he'd said to one of them. *What are you trying to do, pull Mommy's hair out?* he'd said to the other.

Those may or may not have been the exact words. But exact verbiage wasn't what mattered.

What mattered was that she'd flat out rejected Spence. She'd made it clear that she was choosing someone else, then let him walk away.

But twelve hours later, she'd awoken with the words "Mommy" and "Daddy" in her head; that night, she'd fallen asleep to the mental image of her and Spence lying in bed singing "The Band Played On" to a sleepy baby. The mental image, and the longing it inspired, dwarfed any and every feeling she'd ever had for David.

She was on the verge of breaking into another bout of sobs, wondering if she'd made the worst mistake of her life, when the bell above the door jingled.

"Laura?" a voice called.

She sat up abruptly.

It was Spence. Spence himself, standing just inside her shop.

"Laura?" he called again in the darkness. "The door was unlocked. Are you here?"

Sitting herself upright on her knees and wiping away a tear, she remained silent as he walked across her unlit store toward the sales counter. He was now less than ten feet away. He still didn't see her, but he also didn't leave. Instead, he leaned against the wall and slid down onto the floor. He put his elbows on his knees and his face in his hands. For at least a minute, he didn't move. Finally, he reached into his pocket and pulled out his phone. The light of the screen illuminated his face as he composed a text. After letting his index finger hover for a few moments, he hit send.

On the floor beside her, her text tone pinged.

He looked up. "Laura?" he said, squinting into the darkness.

"Spence?" she said, stifling a sob.

"Why didn't you answer me? Are you alright?" He rushed over to her. But he stopped about two feet away. His mouth was open, but no words came out.

He turned and put space between them once again, then pressed his palms against his temples, distressed.

"Spence?" she said, suddenly worried.

"Good God, woman, how much longer do you need to keep torturing me?"

Climbing to her feet, she rushed to his side. "Torture you?"

A look of extreme frustration on his face, he gestured toward her body.

And then she remembered. Snow angel. She was practically naked. She automatically crossed her arms in front of her chest. But then she lowered them. It was her longing for Spence, her fantasy of being wrapped naked in his arms, that had compelled her to change into her see-through lingerie in the first place. And now here he was, standing before her.

"I was feeling lonely," she said. "I wanted to feel sexy."

She had chosen not to hide her body from him. And he wasn't hiding his eyes from her body.

After a few moments, he spoke quietly. "Mission accomplished."

They stood there for what seemed like forever, not moving, not speaking, until it started to feel awkward. Finally, she lowered her eyes. "I have a smock in the closet," she said. "Give me a minute to change."

"Okay," he said, barely audible.

She turned and walked to the storage closet, then closed the door behind her. She reached to the left shelf for her smock, but instead found her fingers grazing Spence's neatly folded flannel shirt. She'd forgotten that she'd hidden it here, the one place David would never find it.

As she had so many times before, she brought it to her face. But this time it was to soak up the tears streaming down her cheeks. Resting her forehead against the bare wall in front of her, she tried to cry as softly as possible, using Spence's shirt to muffle the sound.

She heard the door opening behind her, then footsteps walking into the closet, and then the door once again closing. Just barely, she could hear the lock click into place.

A few more quiet footfalls, and then she felt the warmth of a man's body emanating from behind her. Still facing the wall, she opened her eyes. Spence's hands were pressed up against the wall on either side of her head.

She heard his soft voice behind her. "Please don't change for my benefit."

She sniffled, trying to contain her tears. "It was you I was feeling lonely for, Spence," she said. "It was you I wanted to be sexy for."

She felt his fingertips on the sides of her neck, then running through her hair as he pulled out her scrunchie and let her hair tumble over her shoulders. Gently, he placed his hands on her waist and turned her around so that she was facing him.

"C'mere, girl," he said.

As he pulled her in close, she once again felt tears streaming down her face. She didn't know why. She wasn't sad. She wasn't lonely. It was, she suspected, a confused combination of joy at finding herself at last in Spence's arms, and guilt at being so at peace with it.

He put a finger under her chin and lifted her face. She could feel his lips on her forehead, then her eyelids, and then working their way down her cheek. He was tracing the tracks of the tears she was crying for him with his lips, tasting them on his tongue.

His finger tilted her chin up just a little higher, and then his lips were upon hers. He was kissing her. At long last, Spence was kissing her. She wrapped both arms tightly around his waist, kissing him back.

"Spence," she said as she felt another wave of tears coming. "I want to. You know how much I want to. But David—"

"I don't want to talk about David," Spence said. "You're my girl, Laura. Not his."

You're my girl, Laura. She loved the words. She loved the way his voice sounded when he said them. She loved the way he held her when he said it. And she felt almost certain that he was right. She was his girl. And he was her own beautiful boy.

"You sent me a text this morning," she whispered. "But you never finished it."

Taking her left hand in his, he ran his fingertips over her ring finger. Finding nothing there, he heaved a sigh of relief.

"So you heard," she said.

"I heard," he said. "Courtney from the European Expansion team. She sent out a text this morning saying David bought a ring in Amsterdam."

She had to tell him the truth. "I've haven't answered him yet."

He was quiet for a moment, digesting her words. "But you didn't say yes."

"No, Spence," she said. "I didn't say yes."

He brought her bare ring finger to his mouth for a kiss, as if to reserve the vacant space there for himself. "Can we just stay like this for a while?" he said.

She looked up at him. "What if you just kiss me again?" she said. "It's just a kiss, right? A kiss can't do any har—"

Before she even finished her sentence, he was kissing her again. And kissing her and kissing her. She felt his hands caressing her bare skin under her nightie. In turn, she slid her hands beneath his shirt, caressing his back with her fingers. He was warm. He felt wonderful.

"Spence?" she whispered when they finally came up for air. "Can I ask you something?"

His voice was quiet. "You can ask me anything."

She rested her forehead on his chest, eyes down, hiding. She felt shy, but had to ask. She had to know. "Do you think about making love to me?" she said.

She felt him take a deep breath. "It's all I think about," he said. "Do you think about making love to me?"

"You're driving me out of my mind," she whispered. "I can't sleep. I can't finish a thought. I can't do anything."

He pulled her in tighter. "Laura—"

"Tell me," she said. "Tell me what you think about when you think about making love to me."

She could feel his heart begin to beat more rapidly. "I wouldn't even know where to start."

"Anywhere. Tell me anything. What position do you picture us in?"

Once again, his finger lifted her chin. He kissed her, a little more softly this time. "All of them," he whispered.

This time it was her heart that started racing. She didn't know what answer she had expected, but no answer could possibly be better than the one he had just given her.

"Which position is your favorite?" she asked.

His lips crept down to her neck. "It's a secret."

If he was trying to drive her out of her mind, it was working. She had to know. "Tell me something you picture in your mind. I want to imagine it along with you."

He lifted his head. For a moment he just stood there, his hands loosely holding her waist, as if debating whether or not to comply with her request.

Then, his hands still on her waist, he turned her around so that they were both facing the dusty mirror. The light emanating from the nightlight was dim, but she could see his reflection looking very longingly at her near-naked body.

"We're in the blue bedroom at Powell House," he began. "You're standing in front of the antique mirror. I walk up behind you. You're wearing a robe." His soft lips tickled the side of her neck. "It's silky. And sexy. I untie the belt."

She could feel a very healthy erection pressed up against her backside as she watched him insert his hands up the side of her nightie, then slide his open palms over her stomach until his fingertips were grazing the lacey top rim of her panties. She never realized before just how big he was, and how tiny she was in comparison. The top of her head barely reached his collarbone, and his broad chest and shoulders extended well beyond her slight frame. He was big. He was strong. And with his big hands exploring her little body, he was terribly, terribly sexy.

"Your robe opens," he continued, "and I pull it off your shoulders. All you're wearing now is your panties."

He let his hands move up her stomach until his index fingers were pressed up against the undersides of her breasts and his thumbs were at the sides. He pushed her breasts together. She could feel him shuddering behind her as he watched his owns hands manipulate her breasts in the mirror without fully touching them.

His hands continued tracing the curved contours of her body until they at last found a resting place on her hips. They both watched in the mirror as he slipped his index fingers through the loops of her thong's side ties. She knew what he wanted to do—tug at the strings and watch her panties fall off her body, then untie the front bow of her nightie so it joined her panties on the floor. He wanted her completely naked.

With his fingers still entangled in the loops of her side ties, she let her own hands crawl up her torso and caress her own breasts under her nightie. It felt good. There could be no real substitute for Spence's hands on her bare breasts, but just caressing them with her own hands and pretending it was his hands doing it, with him watching and knowing what she was thinking, was arousing. And not just for her.

Spence's open hands traveled up her torso, just as hers had before, until they were resting on top of hers. He squeezed down. They both sighed audibly.

He closed his eyes as he continued faux-fondling her breasts, his hands completely covering hers. *This is what Spence's hands look like on my breasts*, she thought. *This is what I look like almost naked in his arms. This is what we look like wanting each other, having each other. Almost.*

She was so wrapped up in the moment that she almost forgot he was supposed to be telling her his fantasy. "All I'm wearing is a pair of panties," she said, reminding him of where he left off. "Keep going."

"I'm holding your breasts in my hands," he said. "And you feel so soft, and I've wanted you for so long, and it's so good. And you like it. You want more."

She nodded. *Yes.*

"Your turn," he whispered.

She was delirious. "Hmm?"

"I told you a fantasy. You tell me one."

She'd spent so many hours dreaming of being tangled up with him in a million different varieties of lovemaking that she suddenly understood his response earlier. *I wouldn't know where to start.* The possibilities were endless. But she decided to go with a fantasy that she strongly suspected they both shared.

She looked at their reflection. His eyes were closed, and his fingers were caressing her hips.

"We've just hiked to the hot springs," she began. "No one else is there. It's a warm night and the moon is full. You're wearing what you were wearing that night. A pair of jeans and a gray shirt, your flannel shirt unbuttoned over it. We're standing on the rocks near the outer pool. You're running your hands up and down my back and kissing me. You grab my behind with both hands and pull me in tight. I can feel your erection pressed up against my stomach. You're making me wet. You're making me want you so bad I can't stand it."

He made one of those sounds that exist purely in the realm of lovemaking—amorphous, indescribable— all you know is that it sounds like desire. He turned her around to face him so that, like in her fantasy, he was holding her body tight against his with his erection pressed up against her stomach.

She continued her narrative as he kissed her cheek, her neck, her shoulders. "You reach up my skirt and caress my thighs. I love the way your hands feel on my bare skin. I want more." Standing on her tiptoes, she brought her mouth to his ear, as if there was someone else in the closet who might hear her. "I ask you if I can take your clothes off," she whispered as she grabbed the collar of his shirt. "You say yes."

He let out a deep breath. Taking that as a sign that he liked the direction of her fantasy, she unbuttoned the top button of his shirt. She hesitated, waiting to see if he would stop her. He did not. She continued unbuttoning.

When she had undone the last button, she pushed his shirt off his shoulders. Bare-chested, he was just as she remembered him from Haven—solid and slender, muscular but naturally so. A real man.

She inserted her fingertips into the front of his pants and unbuttoned the button. "In my fantasy," she said as she grabbed his zipper, "you always like this part."

She pulled down his zipper.

He brought his mouth down to her ear. "I like that part," he whispered.

She tugged at his jeans, and he stepped out of them and kicked off his socks.

"All you're wearing is your boxers," she continued, mixing fantasy with reality. "And all I want to do is touch you. I want to feel every part of you with my hands and taste every inch of you with my tongue. I can't wait to feel your body against mine." She once again stood on tiptoes and brought her mouth to his ear. "You ask me if you can take my clothes off," she said. "I say yes."

Instantly he grabbed her at the waist and pulled her body forcefully against his. He liked the part where her clothes were about to come off. "My turn," he said, eager to proceed with the undressing part of the narrative. "We're standing on the rocks and all I'm wearing is my boxers. You're wearing the yellow sundress you were wearing the first time I saw you. And you look so sexy, just like you did that day. But this time I don't have to pretend I don't notice that you're not wearing a bra. I don't have to sit there and stare at my pencil and pretend you're not the most beautiful thing I've ever laid eyes on. This time I know you're my girl. And I'm so, so happy."

Tears began to well in her eyes again, and she tightened her grip on him as she struggled to contain them. She'd already figured out that Haven wasn't the first time he thought of her "that way." But neither was the time he pretended to not know how to tie a tie, or the day he asked James to leave the meeting so he could talk to her alone. He'd wanted her from that very first meeting, the one where she'd been so caught up in David that the only thing she'd even noticed about Spence was that he looked tired.

She rested her head upon his chest. "Keep going," she said.

"I unzip your dress and it falls off you," he said. "I pull you in close so I can feel your breasts pressed up against my skin, and then I push your panties down. And you're naked. You're naked and you're all mine." He embraced her tightly. No kissing, no caressing. Just holding her. "You're all mine, Laura," he whispered again.

She remained silent, taking a few moments to let his words fill her mind and body. What he wanted from her was exactly what she wanted to be for him. And she wanted him to know it. "I'm naked," she said, holding his face in her hands and lifting her lips to his, "and I'm all yours, Spence." She kissed him, and the tender way he kissed her back told her that he believed that it was true.

She continued the narrative. "I grab your hand and lead you into the spring. We walk down the rocks into the deepest part of the pool. When it gets too deep for me, you pick me up and I wrap my legs around your waist. And it feels so good to be naked and have my breasts pressed up against you in the warm water. You lift me up higher. I feel your mouth on my breast—"

He made that sound again. She hesitated.

"Don't stop," he said, breathless.

"I feel your mouth on my breast. And it's gentle and it's sweet, but it's exciting, too. You carry me over to the far side of the pool where the flat rocks meet the water. You sit down on one of the rocks with your knees over the edge. I stand between your legs."

She sidled down the length of his body until she was on her knees in front of him.

"I pull off your boxers and let them float away," she said, slipping her hands up the sides of his boxers and caressing the bare skin of his hips. Sneaking a furtive glance down, she could see his erection straining under the fabric. Right there, so near to her hands, barely an inch from her mouth. The only barrier between her lips and his bare skin was a thin piece of cotton. So close but yet so far.

"You have an erection," she said, sure he could hear the longing in her voice. "And it's big and it's beautiful and it's all for me." She kissed his stomach with her open mouth. "It's all mine."

She slid her hands around to his backside, the way she would if she actually had him in her mouth. The temptation to make the jump from fantasy to reality was overwhelming; all she needed to do was pull down his shorts just a bit, and she'd have a few sweet seconds to brush his soft skin against her lips, to feel him on the tip of her tongue. The fantasy mingled with the present moment; she was up to her shoulders in the warm spring waters and down on her knees in the storage closet at the same time.

She removed her hands from his boxers. "Your turn," she said.

"No!" he said, emphatic. But then his voice softened. He held her head gently in his hands. "I'm sorry, Laura, I just meant—please don't stop now."

He liked it. He wanted to hear the rest. And she desperately wanted to please him.

Still on her knees, she closed her eyes and wrapped her arms around his hips, allowing herself the one tiny indulgence of laying her cheek against his erection. She could feel him take a deep breath.

"I kiss it," she said, gently rubbing her cheek up against him. "I hold your erection in my hands and I kiss it. Your skin is so soft and I love the way it feels on my lips and fingers. I caress you with my tongue. I can feel every contour."

With that, she turned her face forward, resting her forehead on his stomach. She couldn't resist. Just barely, she let her lips graze his erection over his boxers. Gently, she kissed him over the fabric. Then another gentle kiss. Then another, and then another, until she was peppering him with sweet tiny kisses up and down the length of his erection.

"You feel so wonderful," she said, allowing her lips to part just a little as she continued kissing him over the fabric. "And you are so, so beautiful."

Her lips crawled up to the tip of his erection, and she opened her mouth. The feel of him between her open lips and the sound he made as her tongue ran itself over his boxers were cruel reminders of what she so desperately wanted but could not have. Nonetheless, she continued her narrative.

"You hold my head in your hands," she said, "and push yourself all the way into my mouth." Her own words driving her insane with desire, she brought her mouth to the elastic waistband of his boxers. Just one kiss. That's all she wanted. As she pulled back the elastic with her teeth, Spence tightened his grip on her head. He wanted it more than she did.

But she knew one kiss would never be enough, not for her, and certainly not for him. Her teeth let go of the elastic and it snapped back against his stomach. She had to regain some distance.

She pulled him down so that he was on his knees before her and they were face-to-face. It was agony. She wanted him and he wanted her and she was practically naked and he was practically naked and both of them had been aching for the other's body for months and now here they were on their knees in the dark on a mattress in a room just big enough to make love in but not doing it.

"I think about making love to you all day long, Spence," she said, kissing his forehead. "And then I go home every night and lie in bed naked with your shirt. It feels like you and it smells like you. I get so wet thinking of you that I can feel it dripping down my thighs." She kissed his nose. "I want to feel you big and hard inside me, and I want you to feel me hot and wet against you. I want you to make me orgasm. And I want you to feel me squeezing you so tight it brings you to orgasm. That's what I dream of the most. The moment when you ejaculate inside me. It would be the best thing in the world." She ran her fingers through his hair. "You're such a man, Spence," she continued, kissing his neck. "And it would be so, so satisfying to satisfy you."

She lifted her mouth to his, biting down gently on his lower lip. "It's your turn, Spence," she said. "Tell me about making love to me."

Once again, the closet grew silent. But she had no intention of being the one to break it. She wanted to hear it from him—his fantasy, his words, his beautiful voice telling her the story of him making love to her.

Finally, he placed his hands on her sides and took a deep breath. "It's about nine at night," he began, allowing his fingertips to caress the curved sides of her breasts, "and I'm at the festival. I've been walking around for hours trying to get up the nerve to go see

233

you. Finally I just do it. I walk into the store and I see you running across the room toward me, and then all of a sudden you've got your arms around me. I hold you and I can feel you shaking. I ask you what's wrong and you tell me you thought I wasn't coming. And I feel so bad for not coming earlier, and mad at myself for keeping you waiting. I hold you, but it's crowded and noisy and all I want is to be far away and alone with you. I grab your hand and we sneak out the back door, and then a few minutes later we're at your house. As soon as we shut the door behind us, I grab you and kiss you. I can't wait to be under the covers with you in a warm bed. I want to make love to you so bad I can't stand it."

His eyes were closed, and he was taking long, deep breaths.

She took his hands in hers and brought them to her chest, guiding his fingers to the single bow that held her nightie closed. He toyed with the tie for a few moments, as if unsure he was interpreting her signal correctly. At last he seemed to discern that it was an invitation. He gave a little pull, and the tie came undone.

She lowered her arms, and he pushed her nightie off her body. A second later, his hands were upon her bare breasts. He had a delightful, soft caress that sent a tingling through her whole body. It wasn't fantasy anymore. It was reality. She wrapped both her arms around his head as his mouth latched onto one breast and his hand squeezed the other, driving her insane with longing.

And then suddenly both his hands were on her behind, pulling her tightly against him as he kissed her mouth.

"Spence," she said breathlessly between kisses. "You said you had a favorite position."

"Hmm?" he said.

"I asked you what your favorite position to imagine us in was. You said it was a secret. Tell me."

He grew quiet for a moment, his hot breath against her ear. "Do you remember the first time you took me to Powell House? When we went up to the little bedroom so you could show me the graffiti on the wall?"

"I remember," she said.

"It was too high for you," he said as he kissed her neck. "There was a stepstool. You said, 'Can you give it to me?' I said, 'Where do you want it?' And you said—"

She gasped. He didn't need to divulge any further—she remembered it now, as clear as day. "I said, 'Up against the wall.'"

She imagined him at that moment so many months ago, being suddenly and unexpectedly aroused by an accidental turn of phrase. The image that rose to her mind was a very pleasing one. And just that fast, his fantasy became her fantasy. She pulled his face to hers and kissed him.

"Spence," she said, wanting it so badly she could barely stand it. "I like it. Tell me."

Whatever shyness he may have felt earlier was now completely gone. This time he did not hesitate.

"I'm standing behind you on the stool," he said as his hands caressed her back. "You're standing on the step above mine facing the wall. I can't resist. I start kissing the back of your neck and shoulders, then wrap my arms around your waist from behind. I reach up for your breasts. I'm squeezing them and you're sighing. You like it. But then you turn around to face me and push me back. I step down, and you're looking at me like you want me. You're wearing that white midriff blouse you used to wear on hot days. You start unbuttoning it, and I can see you have a white lace bra on underneath."

Being undressed by a man was one of her favorite parts of foreplay, but in Spence's fantasy, she was disrobing herself. She imagined him lying in bed, night after night, fantasizing about her performing a private strip-tease just for him, and it was insanely exciting. Once again, fulfilling his fantasy became her fantasy.

She listened eagerly as he continued. "You pull off your shirt and let it drop to the floor. You're wearing your purple wraparound skirt with the flowers on it, the one that always slides open at the thigh when you sit down, and when you untie the bow, it falls away. Now all you're wearing is your bra and panties. I can't believe how beautiful your body is. I can't wait to see you naked."

He kissed her. Running his hands up her arms to her shoulders, he continued.

"You push your bra straps over your shoulders. You're teasing me and it's working. I want you like crazy." He ran his fingertips down her spine. "You unhook your bra and now all you're wearing is your panties." His heart pounded against her chest as he ran his hands over the thin satin side ties of her thong. "I want to take them off you."

The room grew silent.

"Please don't tease me, Spence," she whispered, her open lips just inches away from his. "Tell me the part where you take off my panties."

"I grab you at the waist and pull you against me," he said as he slid his fingertips under the sides of her thong. "I tug at the strings and your panties fall off. I lift you up and you wrap your legs around me as I carry you over to the wall."

She shuddered in his arms. She thought of all the times she pictured herself with her legs wrapped around him, of all the times she had lain in bed at night naked but for his flannel shirt, caressing her inner thighs with her fingertips and imagining it was his hips rubbing up and down between her legs as he made love to her.

"Spence," she said, "maybe you could just hold me like that for a few minutes. You could pick me up and I could wrap my legs around you and we could pretend—"

She had barely finished uttering the word "pretend" than he was springing to his feet and bringing her along with him. A split second later her back was pressed up against the closet wall and her legs splayed wide, held open by the force of his hips against hers. His hands were gripping her behind, and she could feel his thumbs tracing the bottom-most ridge of her panties. She bit down on his shoulder as she pressured her hips forward against his stomach.

"Oh my God," he said, breathless.

"Spence?"

"You're wet. I can feel you. Even through your panties I can feel you."

Suddenly his hands were grabbing her thighs, and he began pushing her body up, up, up the wall, until her open legs were at the height of his collarbone. He gave one last push upwards, then pressed one of her thighs flush against the wall and positioned the other one over his shoulder.

As he began sucking on the underside of her thigh just at the rim of her panties, her desire for him morphed into delirium. She desperately wanted to feel his fingertips caressing her wet flesh, even if just for a moment. *Just do it,* she thought. *Please just do it.*

As if reading her mind, his finger began toying with the bottommost ridge of her panties. She grew eager as she felt the elastic separate from her skin, and then Spence's finger sneaking under the fabric.

The next sound that emerged from his throat was almost a gasp. She had told him she wanted him to feel how wet he made her, and now here he was, feeling for himself how very much she wanted him. As he massaged her back and forth, she closed her eyes, almost crazed with desire.

It was then that she felt his hot breath between her legs, followed by his mouth closing in for a kiss. Like the touch of his hands, the touch of his lips was soft and tender but wildly exciting, and suddenly she understood the expression "turned on" at a level so deep it was almost primal. It was as if Spence had found a deeply buried switch, flicked it on, and ignited a dormant light source, one that was suddenly shooting through her whole body. She wanted him from the core of her being to the tips of her toes. She wanted him in her veins. She wanted him inside her.

And she wanted to tell him what she was feeling. But when she opened her mouth to speak, the words that came out were much simpler.

"Hey, boy," she said.

He looked up at her, silent.

"It's been six months. How much longer are you going to keep me waiting?"

As her fingers reached down to her panties to grasp the string tie on her left hip, Spence's fingers reached up and grasped the string tie on her right. They each gave one quick tug. The bows came untied, and her panties fell off her body onto the floor.

She was naked. After so many months of longing and dreaming and waiting, she was naked for her beautiful boy. Spence began kissing her stomach, her breasts, her neck as he lowered her down the wall. When her hips were once again at the level of his stomach, she wrapped her legs loosely around him. As he leaned in for a kiss, he spoke only one word. "Laura."

Holding her against the wall with his hips, he pulled off his boxers, and she reached down and found what she'd been aching for these last long months. With one hand she caressed the tip of his erection, luxuriating in the feel of his skin on her fingertips, while her other hand squeezed him tight. The sound he made as he pushed his hips upward was one of pure desire, and she could feel his erection pressing against her wet skin. Her hands let go of him. And then there it was—that nirvanic moment of penetration, an overwhelming thrill as Spence plunged into her.

She gasped at the feeling of him inside her, bigger than she'd dreamed and harder than she could have hoped for. And from the gratified sound that came out of his throat at his first thrust, she knew he could feel her too, tight and warm and dripping wet for him.

He began moving slowly in and out, and in response she pushed her hips forward against him. Within a few strokes, they were moving together in perfect rhythm. Her mind floated in a state of near-disbelief. *Spence is naked in my arms. Spence is inside of me. Spence is making love to me.* She took his face in her hands, her fingertips shaking.

"Spence," she said, "kiss me."

He leaned down. The feel of his soft lips on hers sparked a tremor deep inside her, and he gasped as she tightened around him. Her pleasure was feeding his pleasure, and as his pleasure increased, so did his pace. She felt her walls closing in, not yet at climax, but sufficient to make her sigh audibly and to elicit an "Oh my God" from Spence.

At the sound of his words, the desperate desire to please him that had been building all night approached its apex. She pushed her hips hard against him, setting off another tremor, this one more intense than the one before. After another moan, his pace increased again, this time to a speed she could not keep up with. She wrapped her arms tightly around his neck. It was all him now.

He continued his thrusts, smooth and relentlessly hard, stroking and stoking the walls inside her. She felt her climax approaching, and she could tell from his hitched breathing that he could feel her coming close.

She felt a tremor, then another, and then another. And then it came—an intense spasm that sent a shockwave through her entire body. He felt it, too. As her spasm continued, he made one final thrust, one final sound of joy, and climaxed inside of her.

Still holding her, he stumbled over to the mattress. After dropping to his knees, he eased them into a sitting position. Wrapped up arm and leg with him on the floor, with him still inside her and his heart beating against hers, she was overcome by a new and strange sensation. Spence was coursing through her veins. He was tingling in her fingers and toes. He was the salt in the tears that were running down her face.

And all at once, she understood what was happening. She'd heard it spoken about at church every Sunday for the whole of her life, but had never really experienced it. But here it was, and it was deep and full and profoundly real.

Communion.

She lifted her head from his shoulder and looked up at him. "Spence," she heard her trembling voice say, "you love me."

He laid his lips on her forehead, eyes still closed. "You love me, too, Laura."

As he held her in his embrace, her mind traveled back to the night of their hike to the hot springs, when she had watched him gaze out at Granite Mountain, his face crisscrossed with light and shadow, the last rays of pink sunlight reflecting off his hair. What she had suspected that night, she was absolutely certain of now: there was nothing in the world so beautiful as a beautiful boy, and if she lived a hundred years, she would never again love anyone or anything more sweetly and completely. After months and months of uncertainty, there was no longer a shred of doubt in her mind. She was madly, ecstatically, rapturously in love with Spence Markham.

He ended their night as he had started it, lifting her chin with his finger and tracing the tracks of her tears with his lips. "Laura," he said, kissing her mouth. "My girl."

She held his face in her hands, kissing him back. "My beautiful boy."

CHAPTER 19

It was a tiny sliver of sunlight creeping under the door that woke her up. It took her a moment to orient herself. She was on the floor of her store's supply closet on a camping mattress. A man's arm was around her waist, and she could feel his stomach rising and falling against her back.

Spence. He was sound asleep, his naked body spooning hers.

Careful not to wake him, she rolled over to face him. He was lovely when he was sleeping. Or maybe just lovely sleeping beside her. He looked peaceful, like a man content in the knowledge that the woman in his arms loved him and only him.

Or so she imagined. Maybe she only wanted to believe that the uncertainty of the past few months was all behind them now. He'd made it very clear to her on Friday night that he could no longer just "sit there and take it" when it came to her relationship with David. There could be no more back and forth. It was David or Spence. And while she'd evidently had very little trouble cheating on David, the thought of breaking the bond with Spence was inconceivable.

She still had to tell David it was over. And she had to do it soon. As in today. She'd drive to his apartment this afternoon and be waiting for him when he got home from work. It was going to be awful. She still loved David—he was a good person with a good heart, kind and loving and trusting and forgiving and about a million other adjectives that unfortunately made him more vulnerable to hurt than others. After over a quarter of a century of observing human nature, Laura knew that the kinder and more loving a person was, the more deeply they felt the pain of betrayal. Not only had David forgiven her for the hot tub incident, he had taken her at her word when she said there was nothing between her and Spence. He had never mentioned it again, and had never again shown any sign of jealousy or suspicion. His faith in her was unwavering.

And undeserved. Not only had she slept with another man, she had done it the same day David asked her to marry him. And she only had twelve hours to figure out a way to break it to him. Lying would be the kinder path, but it wasn't an option. David and Spence worked together. And as Laura had learned over the last several months, KPS was an office that loved its gossip. There was no way she and Spence would be able to keep their new relationship a secret. It was better that David heard it from her than via another company-wide text that potentially featured the word "blowjob."

Carefully lifting Spence's arm off her waist, Laura crawled off the mattress and tiptoed over to the shelf to grab her sweats. She quickly dressed, then scribbled a quick note to Spence to meet her at the house when he woke up.

Ten minutes later she was stepping through her front door and locking it behind her. Spence had a key, he could let himself in.

She had only made it three paces into her house when she saw him. He was sitting on the couch, fully dressed and wide-awake.

"David," she said, nervously walking into the living room. "What are you doing here?"

So much for her plan of taking the day to think about how she was going to tell him. The fact that he was here, sitting on her couch at seven o'clock in the morning but refusing to look at her, told her that he already had a very good idea of what was going on.

He reached over to the end table and grabbed his phone. "I got an exciting message from James last night," he said. "You want to hear it?"

She said nothing.

He hit play and pressed the speaker button.

"Hey, David," James's panicked voice said, "I don't know if you heard, but Spence sent in his resignation three hours ago and he's not answering anyone's calls. Camille's going nuts and calling me every fifteen minutes asking where he is like I'm his goddamned babysitter or something. I'm here alone with the kids, so can you please drive over to Spence's and try to talk some sense into him? I'm not supposed to tell anyone this, but I caught him and Laura hugging the other night and Laura was crying and when I asked Spence if the rumors were true, he said yes, and I'm thinking that's why he quit so suddenly, so he could quit before Camille had a chance to fire him. But please just go to his house and tell him to just go to HR and sign a disclosure. The campaign's over and he and Laura can live happily ever after for all anyone cares. But the whole Amsterdam campaign's built around him, and if Spence goes, so does Amsterdam and—goddammit, Camille's calling me again. Just please go over there and talk some sense into him. Call me when you get this, bye."

The message ended, and David laid his phone facedown on the coffee table. "Well?" he said.

It was the moment of reckoning. There was no way out of it. After months of flip-flopping, the time had come for her to take responsibility.

She walked over to the couch and sat down next to him. He didn't look at her.

"Everything James said is true," she admitted. "Spence and I were hugging Friday night, but that was because I was saying goodbye. I swear we never had any kind of relationship, just a kind of mutual crush, but I was saying goodbye because I was choosing you."

"You're sure about that?" David said. "Because I've been here alone since eleven o'clock last night, you *haven't* been here, and Markham's car is parked in your driveway.

She lowered her head. "I wasn't finished explaining yet," she murmured.

"Please. Tell me more. I can't wait."

"Friday night was goodbye. Spence didn't even come to the festival on Sunday. We were never supposed to see each other again. But then he got a text from Courtney or Cathy or someone saying you bought a ring in Amsterdam and he showed up at the store about nine last night and wanted to know if it was true.

And . . ." This next part was going to be hard. But she spit it out. "And I had to make a choice."

"That's it?" David said, clearly dumbstruck. "You're telling me nothing ever happened between you two except one hug, and then two days later he asks you to choose and *just that fast* you choose him? Did you at least spend thirty seconds thinking about it before you decided to throw away everything we've built?"

"It's a little more complicated than that," she said, looking away.

"Do I even want to hear what you mean by 'complicated'?"

"No, David," she said. "I don't think you do."

He sat quietly, processing her words. "His car's still in the driveway," he finally said. "Where is he?"

"At the store," she said. "He's sleeping. But this is all on me, David. Spence never made you any promises. I did. I'm the one you should be mad at."

"Don't worry, I'm plenty mad at you, but I also have plenty reason to be mad at Markham. What you don't know is that in addition to screwing my girlfriend, he—"

The sound of a door opening interrupted him. David jumped to his feet when he saw Spence walking into the room.

"Why the hell do you have the keys to her house?" he snapped.

Spence was in the entryway, closing the door. He looked calm, but he had to have seen David's car. He had to have known what he was walking into.

"I installed the locks," he said to David. "I forgot to give Laura the spare keys."

David walked toward Spence. "Let me take those off your hands for you," he said. He waited, hand outstretched, palm upright.

Spence looked to Laura, and she nodded yes. He dropped the keys into David's palm.

"Thank you," David said. "Is there anything else we can help you with today? Did you need to fuck my girlfriend again before you go back to KPS and fuck over everyone there, too?"

"David—" Laura began.

"Laura," David said, "I don't think you fully appreciate what's going on here. Yesterday morning I came home thinking I was going to get a hundred-thousand-dollar commission that my fiancée and I could use as a down payment on our first house. And less than twenty-four hours later, I'm not only losing the woman I love, I'm losing my hundred-thousand-dollar commission because the whole Amsterdam deal that James and I have been working on for *three months* was built around the one and only Spence Markham leading the creative team. If Spence goes, so does the Amsterdam deal. And it's not only me he's screwing over. You do know that Bethany is pregnant with babies four and five, right? James's base salary is only eighty thousand dollars a year. Do you have any idea how much he needs the Amsterdam commission? Do you see what Spence is doing to his own sister and brother-in-law?"

"You know what, David?" Spence interrupted, his voice angry. "Bullshit. You and James and everyone else at KPS knows that I've wanted out for years. This is the fifth time in six years that I've tried to quit, and every time I get guilt-tripped into staying. 'You can't quit, Spence, we just signed with the cruise line and if you leave, Miles won't be able to pay for his wedding.' 'You can't quit during the Empire campaign, Spence, Sally just bought a house in the suburbs and she won't be able to pay for the down payment.' 'Oh, didn't you hear, Spence, Bob's daughter got accepted to Yale—if you quit now, he won't get his commission on Harbinger and she'll have to go to community college and it will be all your fault.'"

He took a deep breath. "Well, you know what, David? It's not my fault that my brother-in-law can't walk through the front door and say, 'Honey, I'm home' without getting my sister pregnant. I'm not going to spend another ten years of my life at a job I hate so James can support his wife and his family and his four-bedroom house and all the things I *don't* have because I'm working seventy hours a week to support *him*. Sally has her dream house, Bob's daughter is at Yale, James gets to be father of the year in the house whose down payment *I* paid for, and I don't have shit because I have to work night and day so everyone else at KPS can have a normal life. So if you think I'm just going to sit here and say, 'Okay, I'll spend another ten years at KPS so David can use the commission he made selling *me* to the city of Amsterdam to marry Laura, you're out of your mind."

Spence turned to Laura. "Laura, I'm sorry for yelling, I'm sorry for swearing, I'm sorry for talking about you like you're not here. I know this is your decision. But I finally have a chance to have a real life and a real future and I'm not voluntarily giving it all up so that David can have it instead of me." He turned his attention back to David. "I'm leaving KPS no matter what Laura decides. Marielle and Hector are perfectly capable of doing a great job on Amsterdam. I'm sorry for whatever financial hardship anyone incurs in the short term, but I'm not backing down this time. My decision is final. I'm done."

"Believe it or not, Markham, I wasn't actually looking forward to seeing you at work every day for the rest of my life, so go ahead and quit. I think I'll recover emotionally. But at the moment my girlfriend and I have some very important matters to discuss and the opinions of outsiders aren't welcome, so why don't you just get in your car, drive to the office, collect your stuff, and get the hell out of everyone's life?"

Spence turned to Laura. "Do you want me to go?" he said.

Eyes down, she nodded.

"Okay," he said. "I'm sorry about all this. The yelling—"

"She said you can go now."

He gave Laura a nod, then mouthed, *I'll call you.*

"No, you won't!" David yelled as Spence walked toward the front door.

The doorknob clicked, and Spence was gone.

David returned to the couch, sitting beside Laura with about a foot of awkward space between them. She looked down at her lap. There was only one thing she could think of to say.

"I'm sorry, David. I'm sorry for hurting you. I'm sorry for betraying you. I don't expect you to forgive me. I expect you to hate me and I don't blame you. I kind of hate myself right now." She spoke with sincerity, even though she had no expectation of being believed or forgiven.

"I don't hate you, Laura" he said. His voice was calmer now. "I'm mad. I'm hurt. But I don't hate you. If you want to know the truth, I think part of this is my fault. If I hadn't given you the ring, Courtney never would have sent out that text and Markham wouldn't have come running here—"

"No," she said almost angrily. "No way. You don't get to blame yourself. For anything. This is all on me and the ring had nothing to do with it. And even if it did have something to do with it, it still wouldn't be an excuse for what I did."

David did not respond, and Laura could think of nothing else to say that wouldn't somehow end up being hurtful. So they sat there. And sat there and sat there. After about ten minutes of silence, she glanced over to him.

His eyes were closed. He was thinking. About what, she had no clue.

"Laura?" he finally said. "Do you still love me?"

"Yes," she said, her response immediate and emphatic. "Yes, David, I still love you."

"Then why did you do it?"

The honest answer to that question was *Because I'm in love with Spence.* But she was pretty sure honesty was not the best policy at this particular moment. "I don't know," she said. "I'm sorry I don't have a better explanation than that. I don't know why and I don't know what to do next."

He moved in a few inches closer to her, but stopped at touching her. "I don't think either of us knows what to do right now," he said. "But I think we can both start by not making any rash decisions."

She couldn't believe what she was hearing. If she wasn't mistaken, David was suggesting that this didn't have to be the end.

"If you'd never met Markham," he said, "what would have happened?"

"If I hadn't met him?" she said, confused. "Nothing would have happened."

"That's my point," David said. "If it weren't for him, would there be anything wrong between us right now?"

"Of course not," she said. "There was never anything wrong between us, David. I know what I've done, but please don't think it was because there was anything lacking in you. You're good and kind. Loving. Trusting. Patient. And our relationship has been as close to perfect as possible. We don't argue. You make me laugh. The sex is spectacular. What happened had nothing to do with you as a person or us as a couple."

"That's exactly my point," David said. "Take him out of the picture and there's nothing wrong. We love each other. We're happy." His next words were firm. "We understand each other, Laura. We're right for each other. The one and only thing standing in the way of a long and happy life together is him."

She was taken aback. David was right. If it weren't for Spence, she would have said yes the minute David proposed. They would have gotten married and bought a house and had a family and lived happily ever after.

She hadn't ended up in bed with Spence because she and David were wrong for each other. She ended up in bed with Spence because she was in love with two men at the same time. When she woke up this morning in Spence's arms, her choice had seemed so clear. Now, with Spence gone and David here reminding her of all they'd built together and all they had in one another, she wasn't so sure anymore.

"David?" she said.

"Yes?" he said.

"Do you remember the night we first made love?"

For the first time all morning, he allowed himself to smile, just a little. "Of course I remember."

"You'd been totally stressed because of work for about two weeks. You had insomnia every night. Then we made love. I made your favorite dinner. We made love again. That night you slept for ten hours straight and you didn't talk about work all weekend. You were so happy. And I was so happy that you were happy. And I remember thinking that this was the kind of person I wanted to be for you. I'm supposed to take care of you. When everyone else lets you down, I'm supposed to be the one person who doesn't disappoint you. I'm the one who's always supposed to make you feel safe."

"Laura," he said, taking her hand. "You are that person."

"Are?" she said. "Or were? David, I don't think all this has really sunken in yet. It's so much more than me spending the night with someone else. It's more than just a question of whether or not you can forgive me. We had a bond and I broke it. Do you really think that this is just a wound that will heal over? Do you really think we can just get on with our life like none of this ever happened?"

She could tell by the look on his face that she had made her point. Even if he could forgive her, should he? Could the bond she had broken ever really be glued back together?

"You might be right, Laura," David said. "I don't think it's fully hit me yet. And I don't know if I'm thinking clearly right now. But the fact that you just said 'our life' in the singular makes me feel a little hopeful."

He took both her hands in his. She laid her head on his shoulder, and he laid his head on top of hers.

"So what do we do now?" she said.

He squeezed her hands. "I think we need some time apart," he said. "I don't want it, but I think we need it. Clear our heads. Figure out what to do."

"I think you're right," she said. "And I know what you're thinking, and I'm not going to turn around and call him as soon as you walk out the door. I promise, David. I just want to think about us and what we need to do."

He gave her hand one last squeeze and stood up. When they were at the front door, he embraced her.

"I love you, Laura."

He'd said it a million times before, and it still gave her shivers.

"I love you, David," she said, wrapping her arms tightly around him. "That's the one and only thing I know for sure right now. No matter what happens, I hope you believe me when I tell you that's the one thing that never, ever changed."

He gave her one last kiss on the forehead, and he was gone.

She didn't go to the window to watch him as he walked away. This could be the end or it could be the beginning. And if it was the end, she didn't want her last memory of David to be of him with his back to her, walking away forever. She wanted to remember his last embrace, and more importantly, his last words.

She went to the bedroom and laid her head down on his pillow, feeling more exhausted than she ever had in her life. As she drifted off to sleep, she knew that there were only two possible outcomes to what had transpired over the course of the last twenty-four hours.

Either she was going to marry David, or they'd just said "I love you" to one another for the last time.

CHAPTER 20

Laura looked out her window at the first snowfall of the season. Winter had arrived late, and it was the first year in ages that North Powell hadn't had a white Christmas. But at least they were having a white Boxing Day. She supposed that was something.

Her phone rested on her lap. Although she'd desperately wanted to call him for weeks now, she kept finding reasons to put it off. *It's too soon.* Being impetuous was what had gotten her into this mess in the first place. She needed to prove to him that she could be trusted to make well-thought-out, rational decisions. *It's the middle of the holidays.* He was probably busy and wouldn't be able to make time for her. He'd given her time to think. But in giving her time to think, he had given himself time to think as well. He was the rational one. If he was smart—and he was—he'd turn tail and run.

But whatever his decision, she needed to know. It was five days before the end of the year. If his answer was goodbye forever, getting over him and moving on with her life would be her New Year's resolution.

She pulled up her contacts and pressed his name. The phone rang three times, then four, then five. She wondered if he was purposefully not answering. For all she knew he had already deleted her from his contacts.

But just as she was about to hang up, she heard his voice. "Hey," he said.

"Hey," she said back. "It's Laura."

She heard him laugh a little. "I know who it is."

He sounded happy to hear from her. Or so she chose to believe. "How've you been?" she asked, letting her guard down just a bit.

"Pretty good, all things considered. I had a lot to think about. But good. You?"

"Same."

Silence followed. The ball was in her court, and she needed to move the conversation forward. "So listen," she began, her nervousness returning, "I know this is kind of last-minute and you probably already have plans, but on the off chance you're available, I wanted to know if you were busy New Year's Eve. St. Martin's has a really nice annual dinner dance. It's alcohol-free and ends at nine, but other than that it's a total blowout bash. Free cupcakes and everything."

He laughed. "Free cupcakes and then to bed by nine thirty," he said. "I'm not sure I can handle all that excitement."

"Oh," she said, "I totally get it if you already have plans. Or just don't want to come. It's last-minute and most people want to ring in the New Year with something a little stronger than lemonade—"

"Laura?" he said.

"Yeah?"

"I'm joking. I'd love to come."

She tried to hide her smile, then realized he couldn't see her face anyway.

"What time should I be there?" he asked.

"It depends on how hard you want to party," she said. "Opening prayer is at six. The dance starts at about 6:15 and then the potluck starts at seven. It's not too late to back out if you think your heart can't take the excitement."

"Well," he said, "I hate to admit it, but what you just described sounds way more entertaining than anything I've done for New Year's Eve in the last three years. I'll try to be there at six, but I might hit traffic, what with ski season and all."

"It's fine if you're late," she said. "I'll see you when you get here."

"Sounds like a plan," he said.

They said their goodbyes, and the call was over. She laughed a little at herself. Over the course of the last three weeks, she'd spent many a sleepless night driving herself insane worrying about the outcome of the phone call she'd just made. Suddenly all her paranoia seemed incredibly silly.

Five more days. She couldn't wait.

CHAPTER 21

On New Year's Eve, Laura made sure to sit in the very back row of the church at the far end of the pew. If he miraculously got here on time, she wanted to make sure he could easily spot her.

She put her purse down next to her, reserving a seat for him, then checked her traffic app. The single-lane mountain road to North Powell was clear, but the interstate was backed up for miles. It was possible he wouldn't get here until after the dance was almost over.

"Please rise for the opening hymn," Reverend Smith said.

The congregation rose. Laura spotted her mom standing in the choir's second row with all the other altos. The organist began playing, and Laura opened her hymnal even though she'd known all the words by heart since she was about two.

She began singing with the congregation.

> *Great is Thy faithfulness*
> *Morning by morning new mercies I see*

She felt an elbow nudge her.
"Hey," he whispered.

She felt her heart begin to race. The old adage was true—absence did make the heart grow fonder. He had never looked so handsome.

The reverend began her yearly "go forth into the new year with grace and goodness" speech, but Laura wasn't listening to the mini-sermon. Her attention had been stolen away by the feel of him taking her hands in both of his. She closed her eyes as he brought them up to his lips and kissed them. He was really here. And he was happy to see her. The past was in the past. It was New Year's Eve, and this was their new beginning.

She hadn't longed to escape a church service this much since she was five years old. But it wasn't a service, it was just a pre-party hymn and blessing, and within five minutes the congregation was filing out of the pews and making their way to the dining hall for the biggest social event of the season.

"So where to now?" he said as they followed the crowd.

"This way," she said, grabbing his hand and heading toward a room down the church's long hallway. "There's someone who wants to say hello to you."

They were just a few doors down from Room 4 when she saw her mom walking out of it and heading toward the kitchen.

"Mom!" Laura called over the noisy crowd. "Wait up!"

Her mom turned, stepping out of the crowd so Laura could catch up.

When the rest of the congregation had flowed into the dining hall, they at last found themselves in relative silence. She let go of his hand.

"Mom," Laura said, gesturing to her guest, "this is Spence Markham. Spence, this is my mom."

Her mom gave Spence her trademark smile. "It's so nice to finally meet you, Spence," she said, shaking his hand in her ever-so-ladylike manner. "I'd ask you a little about yourself, but Laura hasn't stopped talking about you for a month. How's that cut on your left ankle, by the way?"

"She really has told you a lot," Spence said. "It's finally all healed, but I think it's going to leave a scar."

"Well," her mom said, "that's what you get for not wearing proper work boots when removing floorboards. I see you finally got new sneakers, by the way. It's about time. Those old gray Nikes looked like something salvaged from a dumpster."

For a brief moment, Laura felt embarrassed that her mom had spilled her secret that she hadn't stopped talking about him for a month. But at the same time, she was glad. Now he knew that there had been no long nights agonizing over her decision, no tortured emotional struggle about who to choose. It was Spence. She'd figured that out about two minutes after she texted him to say she needed some time alone to think. The only reason she'd waited so long was that she felt like she owed it to David to put at least a few weeks of mourning between the end of their relationship and the start of her new one.

She'd had no idea how she was going to break the news to David, but he had solved that problem for her. The day after Christmas, he had called to tell her it was over. He said he wasn't angry, but he had realized that she was right. It had nothing to do with anger or hurt or forgiveness. The bond was broken. What they'd had together was gone and it was never coming back. It was time for him to move on. She got the impression that he wasn't completely over her yet, but she wasn't completely over him either. Still, he was moving on with his life, and it was time for her to start moving on with hers. That same evening, she called Spence and invited him to the New Year's dance.

And here he was.

"Oops! Gotta start setting up for dinner, let's talk more later," her mom said, and disappeared into the kitchen.

Spence turned to Laura and gave her a fake look of offense. "Salvaged from a dumpster?"

"You'll have to pardon my mother," Laura said. "I believe the words I *actually* used were 'salvaged from a dumpster.'"

As the first dance song of the night—slow with a distinct electric guitar vibe—began playing from the dining hall, she smiled. "Ready to party?"

He raised one eyebrow. "Is this an eighties dance?"

"If you mean is the music of the night eighties-themed, then yes. If you mean are half the people here tonight at least eighty years old, then also yes."

He laughed. "It'll still be the most exciting thing I've done for New Year's Eve in three years."

They walked into the dining hall as one slow song ended and another began. Spence pulled her in close to him on the dance floor, and for the next five minutes they swayed in a tight embrace like two lovesick teenagers on prom night, 1983. It felt wonderful to be in his arms again.

The song drew to a close. The slow-dance intro to New Year's Eve was over, and now it was time to party North Powell style. As a high-energy eighties song began to play, everyone in town over forty-five stormed the dance floor, ready to embarrass their kids and grandkids with their old-people dance moves.

Spence brought his mouth to her ear. "I desperately want to be alone with you," he said. "How do you feel about getting out of here early?"

She smiled. "I think I can be persuaded."

He took her hand and they headed back to the sanctuary. Putting on their coats, they walked out the front door.

"Oh, shoot," Laura said just as they reached the bottom of the steps. "I didn't tell my mom we were leaving. Do you mind if I run back in for a sec?"

"Sure," he said. "I'll be right here."

"Be right back."

She ran in, found her mom, said a quick goodbye, and then ran back out to find Spence standing alone in the corner of the churchyard, seemingly checking out the architecture.

She walked over to him. "It's a beautiful church, isn't it?"

"It is," he said. "Do you know who designed it?"

"Of course I do," she said, taking his hand and leading him to the front right corner of St. Martin's. She pushed her way through the shrubs and squatted down. Spence squatted beside her.

"Right here," she said, pushing aside some dead leaves to reveal the marble cornerstone. "Randall Sweeney Welsh. Heard of him?"

"No," Spence said, fingering the "1878" carved into the marble. "Is he a big deal?"

"I think so," she said. "He designed the state capital building and at least one of the museums in the city. And a bunch of libraries. St. Martin's has been landmarked since my mom was a kid, so yeah, I'm pretty sure he's a big deal as architects go."

Spence stood back up, then pushed his way back through the shrubs and returned to the front of the church. He stood about twenty feet from the front door, a serious look on his face. "What year did you say Powell House was built?" he asked her.

"I was never able to find the original architectural plans, but anecdotally it's said to have been 1886. A year after the town was incorporated."

He continued standing there, arms crossed in front of his chest, tapping his elbow with his fingertips.

"Are you going to make me guess what's going on in that head of yours or are you going to tell me already?"

He walked over to the right side of the steps and pointed. In contrast to the church's ornate façade, the steps were rectangular and utilitarian but for one unique feature. A single rose was carved on the top step.

"Rose was his daughter," Laura explained. "She died when she was seven. Supposedly the reason he made the steps so ordinary compared to the rest of the church was that they were meant to be a tribute to her. Sweet and simple, like Rose. It was kind of his trademark. That's why we've been repairing the staircase every five years for the last ninety years instead of just tearing it down and replacing it."

Arms still crossed in front of his chest, Spence looked at her. "Remember that picture you showed me of Powell House from 1910? Before the wraparound porch was added?"

"Yeah?" she said.

"The top front step had that same carving."

She felt her heart skip a beat as she realized the implications of what he was saying.

He grabbed her hand and they both ran across the parking lot to his Jeep. A few minutes later they were parking outside Powell House, and Spence was crawling under the porch on his hands and knees. Laura ran into the house and grabbed two spades and a flashlight from the tool closet. Once back outside, she crawled under the porch toward Spence and handed him a spade.

"Right here," he said, showing her where to dig.

They began excavating. The ground was partially frozen and it was no easy task, but after fifteen minutes, Laura felt a cold, smooth surface under her fingertips. "Is this marble?" she said.

"I think so," he said. "Let's keep digging."

After another ten minutes, Laura could feel the indentations of what felt like carved lettering in the marble. "Spence?"

"Did you find something?" He crawled over to her side as she shined the flashlight on her discovery. "What's that?"

"It's engraving. The letter R," she said, pointing to the first letter. She pointed to the second letter. "S." Last letter. "W."

He smiled. She smiled.

And they very aggressively resumed their digging.

"Should we be using our hands to dig?" she said. "I don't want to scratch the cornerstone."

"It's marble," he said. "It shouldn't scratch. Just be careful."

It took another ten minutes to uncover the whole cornerstone. But when Laura shined her flashlight on the fully exposed engraving, they knew their calluses and dirty fingernails had been well worth the effort.

R.S.W.
Bertrand Powell Homestead
1876

"I'm seeing it," she said. "But I'm not sure I believe it."

He was smiling. "Do you want to see what else I noticed?"

"There's more?" she said.

He pointed the flashlight straight ahead. About fifteen feet in the distance were the original front steps. They had never been torn down. The wraparound porch had just been erected over top of them. And sure enough, there on the top riser was the very same rose as the rose on St. Martin's top step.

Laura felt a moment of intense pride. This was why Spence was so good at his job, and why he had been such a highly valued asset at KPS. He saw what others did not. He put two and two together when others didn't even realize there was an equation involved.

They crawled out from under the porch and walked through the front door together for the first time in well over a month.

"Home sweet home," Spence said as Laura flicked on the light and turned the heat up to seventy. When she turned around, Spence was staring up at the ceiling and checking out the floorboards and windows, just as he had the very first time she brought him to Powell House.

"Do I dare ask what you're thinking now?" she said.

He stuck his head into the library, the one and only room they had finished, looking at it with as much pride as if it were his firstborn child.

"I'm thinking about what I want to do with the rest of my life," he said.

"Are you going to stay in marketing?" she asked.

"I could," he said as he wandered into the kitchen. "I've worked with a bunch of resorts in Haven and Bainbridge, and when I let them know I quit KPS, they all offered me jobs. So that's a possibility. I've also thought of starting my own little marketing business. Something simple. Local. Nine-to-five."

"Is that really what you want?" she said. "I thought you hated your job."

He shrugged. "It was never the work itself I didn't like. It was the clientele. The pressure, the egos, the power trips. If I could find more clients like North Powell, then yeah, I'd be happy to stay in marketing." He turned to her. "I wouldn't make half of what I made at KPS, though."

"Is that what you think will make you happy?" she said. "A quiet little business working with clients who can barely afford to pay you?"

He nodded. "I do."

"Then I think you should do it."

He pulled her in for a hug. "I can't tell you how nice it is to hear someone tell me to do what makes me happy."

She returned his embrace. "I'd rather you were happy than rich."

"I did have this one other idea about how to make a little on the side," he said. "Not a full-time job or anything. Just an extra source of income."

"Let's hear it."

"Well," he began, "I was thinking of buying a historic house and turning it into a B and B."

"You mean like this one?"

He shook his head. "No," he said. "I mean this one."

She wasn't quite sure she was hearing him right. "You mean *buy* Powell House?"

"I made good money at KPS," he said, "but I never had any time to spend it, so I've got plenty saved up. The way I see it, this place is already kind of ours, don't you think? All we'd be doing is making it official. Make a down payment, pay back the sixty thousand North Powell's already invested in it. Spend however long it takes to restore it to its former glory. By this time next year, it could be home sweet home."

It was a lot to digest. Not just Spence's idea of buying Powell House, but his copious use of words like "we" and "ours." He'd only looked for jobs within driving distance of North Powell. He talked about starting his own marketing firm. Locally. And now he was talking about them buying a twelve-room house together—only now he was calling it "home."

She laid her head on his chest, tightening her grip around his waist. He responded by wrapping his arms around her shoulders and resting his head on hers. She couldn't remember the last time she felt this safe and contented.

"Spence?" she whispered.

"Hmm?"

"Remember how I told you that Haven was the first time I thought of you as more than a friend?

"I remember," he said.

"I was lying," she said. "It was the night we hiked to the hot springs. You were watching the sunset. I was looking at you, and all of a sudden I thought you were the most beautiful thing I'd ever seen, and that I could never love anyone or anything more than you. And then you looked at me, and I felt so embarrassed—I was afraid you knew what I was thinking. But then I realized it was too dark. You couldn't see the look on my face. You had no idea what I was thinking. It was the first time I realized I was in love with you. And you never knew."

He tightened his embrace. She felt his hand cradling her head, his heart beating against her chest.

"I knew," he said. "It's why I held your hand all the way home."